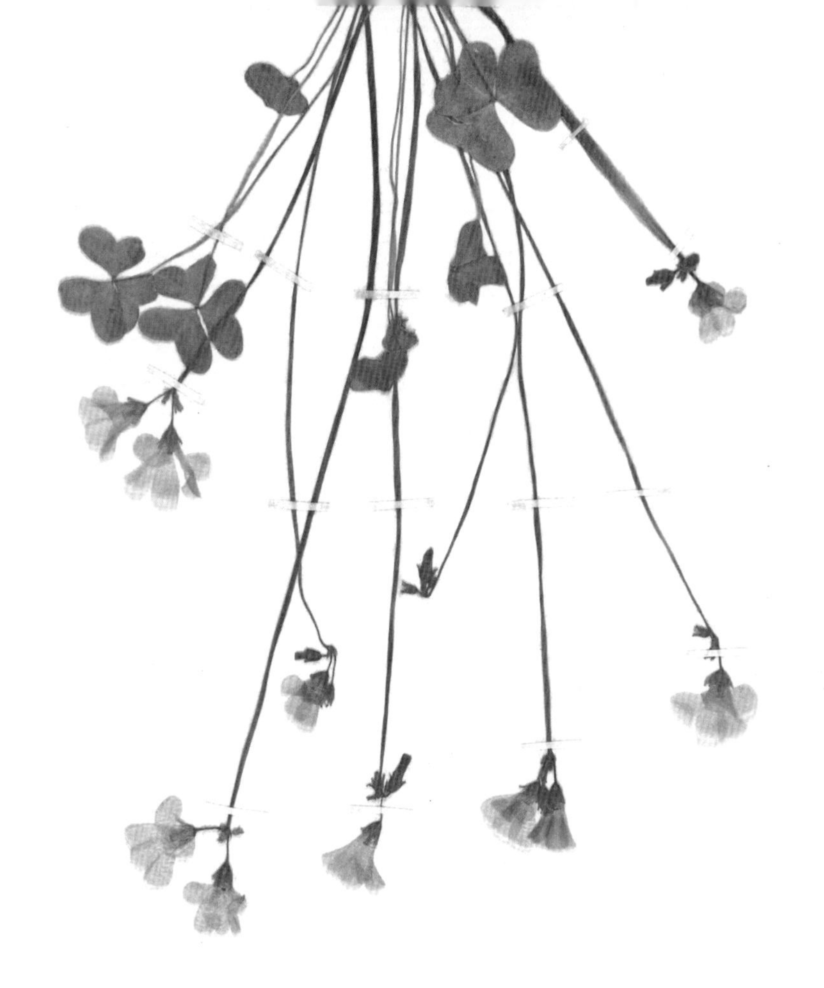

T0161230

PAPER HOUSES

Dominique Fortier
translated by
Rhonda Mullins

Coach House Books, Toronto

First English-language edition. Originally published as *Les villes de papier* by Les Éditions Alto, 2018.

Canada Council for the Arts Conseil des Arts du Canada

Canadä

Coach House Books acknowledges the financial support of the Government of Canada through the National Translation Program for Book Publishing, an initiative of the Roadmap for Canada's Official Languages 2013–2019: Education, Immigration, Communities, for our translation activities. We are also grateful for generous assistance for our publishing program from the Canada Council for the Arts and the Ontario Arts Council. Coach House Books also acknowledges the support of the Government of Canada through the Canada Book Fund.

LIBRARY AND ARCHIVES CANADA CATALOGUING IN PUBLICATION

Title: Paper houses / Dominique Fortier ; translated by Rhonda Mullins.
Other titles: Villes de papier. English
Names: Fortier, Dominique, 1972- author. | Mullins, Rhonda, 1966- translator.
Description: Translation of: Les villes de papier.
Identifiers: Canadiana (print) 20190141107 | Canadiana (ebook) 20190141956 | ISBN 9781552453926 (softcover) | ISBN 9781770566118 (PDF) | ISBN 9781770566101 (EPUB)
Subjects: LCSH: Dickinson, Emily, 1830-1886—Fiction.
Classification: LCC PS8611.07733 V5513 2019 | DCC C843/.6—dc23

Les villes de papier is available as an ebook: ISBN 978 1 77056 610 1 (EPUB) 978 1 77056 611 8 (PDF)

Purchase of the print version of this book entitles you to a free digital copy. To claim your ebook of this title, please email sales@chbooks.com with proof of purchase. (Coach House Books reserves the right to terminate the free digital download offer at any time.)

To Fred and Zoé – my home

To make a prairie it takes a clover and one bee
One clover, and a bee,
And revery.
The revery alone will do,
If bees are few.

EMILY DICKINSON

Emily

Emily is a town built in white wood and nestled amid fields of clover and oats. The square houses have pitched roofs, blue shutters that close as evening approaches, and chimneys that birds sometimes swoop down to fly, frantically, with soot-covered wings, through every room in the house. Rather than being chased out, they are adopted so the residents can learn their song.

The town has ten times as many gardens as churches, and all of the churches are deserted. Bellflowers and mushrooms grow in their tranquil shade. The townspeople speak in signs, but, since everyone uses signs of their own making, they barely understand one another and generally prefer to avoid contact.

In winter, Emily is blanketed in snow, in which learned chickadees write pristine white poems with their dainty feet.

Amherst

Amherst, Massachusetts, is a town – almost a village – out of step with space and time.

When Emily was born, in 1830, the population was 2,631. Chicago didn't exist. By 1890, four years after Emily's death, Chicago's population would be 1,099,850, whereas Amherst had not yet grown to 5,000 souls, minus the one.

It is a cultured little town that has been home to generation after generation of prominent Dickinsons. It was named for Jeffery Amherst, the first baron by that name, the same man who suggested, during the American Indian Wars, giving 'savages' blankets that had been used to warm those suffering from smallpox, to, as he said, extirpate this execrable race.

The town could have picked a better namesake.

These days, as we are assailed by an endless stream of images, it is astonishing to think that only one photograph exists of the woman who was among her country's greatest poets, a photo taken when she was sixteen. In this famous portrait, she looks pale and thin, has a dark velvet ribbon around her long neck; her wide-set black eyes show quiet attention, and there is the trace of a smile on her lips. Her hair is pulled back and parted in the middle. She is wearing a simple striped dress gathered at the waist, with a light-coloured collar, and in her left hand she holds what could be a small bouquet of flowers. A book is set on the table beside her: the title cannot be made out. There are no other photographs that show her younger or older, none where she is elsewhere or standing – or perhaps they have all been lost or destroyed. She has no legs. She never will.

Forever and ever, she will be only this face. This mask.

Emily Dickinson is a blank screen, an empty page. At the end of her life, if she had chosen to wear a blue dress, we would have nothing to say about her.

At age five, little Emily Elizabeth spends a few days at her aunt's in Boston. On the way there, their carriage drives through a violent storm. Lightning rips through the black sky, rain pelts the windows, sounding like gravel. The aunt holds the child to reassure her. But the child is not afraid. Fascinated, she leans toward the cold glass, rests her forehead against it, and whispers, 'Fire.'

At the aunt's house, the windows are set so high up that, even standing on her toes, she can't see anything other than a strip of white sky. She climbs onto her bed to look at the street down below, the twin trees growing across the road, the people scurrying down the sidewalks.

She makes a first tentative jump, then a second, and a third, higher and higher on the goose-down mattress that yields gently under her weight. The street bounces in time with her, with all of its little characters, like toy soldiers being shaken in a box.

'Elizabeth!'

Standing in the doorway, the aunt looks furious. The child immediately stops jumping and, standing tall, planted on her short little legs, answers loudly and clearly, 'Call me Emily, if you please.'

A robin lands on the windowsill where Emily has scattered bread crumbs. His breast is like one of those miraculous oranges that fill the stockings hung from the chimney on Christmas Eve.

He swallows a piece of bread, then tells long bird stories in a series of trills. He tells of worms, a flighty female, a clutch of blue-green eggs, one of which has mysteriously disappeared. Emily listens, quivering, head cocked, eyes bright. She picks up a crumb between her thumb and index finger and brings it to her lips. It is her favourite meal of the day.

When she sins, it is always the same sin: gluttony, which compels her to pinch a slice of the pie that is cooling in the kitchen, a voraciousness that drives her to pilfer the forbidden volume that sits on one of the shelves in Father's study. Mother is never fooled and always punishes her in the same way, by sending her to her room, with no distractions that would amuse children. Once Emily's punishment is over, Mother doesn't notice that her daughter is always sorry to come out. You mustn't know Emily Dickinson very well to think she can be chastised by locking her away in silence, alone with her thoughts.

If she could go one day, just one, with no mischief, bad deeds, or horrid thoughts, her whole life would be redeemed by that single, perfect day. But the fact is, she is not sure she wants to behave. Daisies don't behave, any more than geese do as they fly overhead in a V. They are something better than behaved: they are wild like mustard, they spring unchecked like weeds.

The garden rustles with muttering flowers. A violet hasn't recovered from being badly crushed. Another complains that the large sunflowers cast too much shade. A third eyes its neighbour's petals. Two peonies plot about how to keep the ants at bay. A tall, pale lily has cold feet; the earth is too damp. The roses are the worst, annoyed by the bees, bothered by bright light, drunk on their own perfume.

Only the dandelions are quiet, happy just to be alive.

The flowers the children picked in the afternoon are lying in a wicker basket. Father takes a pansy between his pale fingers and explains in his pastor's voice, 'To preserve them, you need to dry them first.'

In Father's hand, the flower seems to be wilting already. He puts it down and takes out a volume of the *Encyclopædia Britannica*, the set of which stands, ordered 1 to 21, on a shelf in the middle of the bookcase. He opens it, carefully leafing through the pages.

'After a few months, the pages will have absorbed the plant's moisture, and you can glue it in your herbarium.'

Emily is filled with silent wonder: books drink the water of flowers.

Father continues in the learned tone he uses when he is teaching, which is to say, always.

'To remember where you placed the specimen, I suggest choosing a page number that corresponds to a famous date. For example, the date of the beginning of the Hundred Years' War ...'

He waits.

'Thirteen thirty-seven,' Austin, Lavinia, and Emily whisper in unison.

Austin and Lavinia select a volume, gently insert the petals of a flower between the leaves of the book, muttering to themselves, 'Declaration of Independence,' 'Fall of the Roman Empire,' 'Mother's birthday.'

Emily alone seems to scatter flowers at random in the volume she has chosen. Father watches her for a moment, his brow knit.

'How will you find your specimens if you put them just anywhere?'

She smiles.

'I'll find them.'

Months later, when in the dead of winter they pick summer flowers from the bookcase, she opens the dictionary without a moment's thought. While the others mutter numbers, she says a single word, just one, like magic: *jasmine,* and jasmine appears.

Emily has illustrated the dictionary entries.

She picks mint leaves, rose petals, and camomile flowers and gives them to Mother to hang to dry in the kitchen. These plants are not for the herbarium. They are to drink during the winter.

In a small bag, she keeps the seeds snatched from the birds at the end of the summer, the eventual garden.

Mother is in the kitchen; the girls are setting the table for dinner. Father is already seated. At the head of the table, as is fitting, he waits. Lavinia lays out the everyday cutlery, and Emily follows her with the blue-and-white porcelain plates.

Father makes a *tsk* sound as soon as she puts his down.

'Yes, Father?'

'I would like to know why I always get the chipped plate.'

Emily backtracks and squints. It's true: the plate she has placed in front of him is missing a piece, the size of a lunula of a fingernail.

'I'm sorry,' she says.

She picks up the plate and calmly crosses the dining room and the kitchen, opening the door to the garden. There she spots a large, flat rock. She drops the plate on it, and the shards go flying. She goes back in the house with the same measured step and says, 'It won't happen again. I promise.'

Dumbstruck, he doesn't answer.

His reflection on the waxed table is as astonished as he is. In the grass, the shards of porcelain look like the remains of a lost civilization.

'Snow!'

Austin is the first one up. He runs into Emily and Lavinia's bedroom, and Lavinia jumps to the window: the garden is blanketed in white, the trees trimmed with garland.

The three of them race down the stairs to put on their boots, coats, hats, shawls, and mittens. At the foot of the stairs, Father eyes them. He says nothing but is wearing his grandfather-clock expression. The children compose themselves just a little.

No one has been outside yet: they are the first to tramp in the white sheet of the garden, drawing three interconnected labyrinths. They make snowballs that explode like floury firecrackers on their dark coats.

Out of breath, Emily drops onto her back. She flaps her arms, then spreads her legs and brings them back together, to make a snow angel. Austin collapses on her right. Lavinia on her left. A host of angels appears in the snow, like a string of paper dolls.

It is still snowing. The snowflakes burn when they land on the children's rosy cheeks. Their lashes are as white as if sprinkled with icing sugar. When they finally get up, their imprints stay sprawled on the ground – three little recumbent statues in snow.

❧

Years later, leaning out of her window one December morning, Emily sees them again, three little ghosts, age five, seven, and nine. The children are no more, gone as surely as if they had been buried. Years later, looking out at the first snow, she bursts into tears.

❧

In a portrait by Otis Allen Bullard, the children look like variations of the same person (their mother? their father?) – in any case, adults shrunk to childlike proportions: the serious expression, the long nose, the weary smile. They are practically interchangeable, except that Austin is dressed in a little suit with a white collar, while the two little girls are wearing dresses (sea green for Lavinia, a darker shade for Emily) with lace collars. They all appear to have short hair, parted on the side, but the girls' hair may be pulled back. To the modern eye – and perhaps to the eye of the time as well – it could be a painting to remember three departed children, or one that was done years after the brother and sisters grew up, with the adults they had grown into as models.

Because, of course, we know the children survived, grew up, that one of them even had children of their own. Perhaps what the painting shows is that becoming an adult doesn't spare the child from death.

On Main Street, they walk past the grand house built by their grandfather Samuel.

'That's where you were born,' Austin tells Emily.

She knows. They were all born in that house. She refrains from answering, 'And that is where I will die.'

'When grandfather had it built, it was the first brick house in town.'

She knows that too. The big house where she lived until age ten holds no secrets for her, even after – shame, sacrilege, humiliation – Grandfather lost it, and they had to share it with the family of the merchant who bought it. On the west side were the Dickinsons. On the east side were the Macks. Every time Emily encountered one of them in the hallway, she would jump as if she had come upon a ghost or an intruder who had slipped in through the window. What were these strangers doing in her house?

Nearly four years after leaving it, she remembers it down to the last detail: the smell of wax on the blond wood floors, the shaft of sunlight that filtered in through the half-open blinds in Father's office and that made the gold lettering on the spines of the books shine, the murky light of the little milk house where she and Austin would lap the cream off the neck of the milk bottles, the cool cellar fragrant with beets and onions, her bright bedroom.

She knows that the house will be hers again. She is right. In 1855, Emily's father buys the family home and moves the Dickinsons back in, and from that point on, they will occupy all of it. He has the brick painted vanilla and the shutters forest green, in addition to making some improvements, including building a greenhouse where Emily will grow rare plants – another unusual, whimsical pursuit she seems intent on making a specialty.

Going back to Homestead at age twenty-five, she with one stroke erases the previous fifteen years. Now that she is back in her childhood home, she is determined never to leave it again – neither the home nor childhood.

Going back to Homestead at age twenty-five, she thinks, that of all the members of her family, it may be the house she likes best.

For months, I have been rereading Emily Dickinson's poems and letters, consulting scholarly works about her, scouring sites with pictures of Homestead, the neighbouring Evergreens, and the town of Amherst when the Dickinsons lived there. So far, it is a paper town. Is that preferable, or would I write better by visiting the two houses that have been turned into museums? Simply put: is it better to have the knowledge and experience required to describe things as they truly are or the freedom to invent them? Why am I reluctant to make the four-hour drive? When did I become afraid of inhabiting a book? The longer I wait, the more summer wanes. Soon all that will be left of Emily's garden will be dried stems and faded flowers. But maybe that is the way it should be discovered, not in the unbridled lushness of August.

The house where Emily lives from age ten to twenty-five is on Pleasant Street, across from the cemetery. A few times a month, she watches a procession of death pass her window.

Not far from the house, in a clapboard cabin too small to be a barn or a stable, they keep a cow with long eyelashes, Dorothy, that is milked morning and night and that keeps the family in dairy. In a paddock near the cow is a bay horse, Duke, that her father hitches to the carriage when he goes out. The three hens, Gwen, Wren, and Edwig, which lay eggs every other day, cluck in a smaller lean-to, as does a rooster, Peck, fiercely watching over the hens. There is also a pig, which has no name. It is fattened through the summer with table scraps, peels, and cores, and has its throat slit in the fall for sausages, roasts, and chops that last until the new year.

Emily learns a lesson from this: it is important to name things.

On Christmas Day, like all the other days of the year, Edward Dickinson treats his children with a sternness that he hopes is inflected with kindness. Under the fir tree they have trimmed with popcorn garlands, dried apple rings, and paper snowflakes, there is a gift for each child, wrapped in brown paper, tied with a string, as if he meant to mail them and then changed his mind at the last minute.

The children approach one by one, eldest to youngest, to receive an orange and a candy cane, in addition to their gift. The gifts reflect the person who chose them: Edward Dickinson does not believe in spoiling children, even girls. The household has few dolls or stuffed animals and is full of books and prints.

That year, Austin receives a complete, durable, well-made writing set, elegant but not showy: pens, a penknife, bottles of ink, writing paper, envelopes, blotting paper, and a leather desk blotter. He touches the silver tips the same way, in other households, children touch the tip of the bayonet of their toy soldiers.

Emily steps forward, curtseys a little. Father places a hand on her head as a blessing. Mother plants a kiss so light on her forehead that she barely feels it. They give her her gift. The package is long and thin, a tube she tests with her fingers before unwrapping it, careful not to tear the paper. Inside, there is a cylindrical object, two hands in length, its ends – one of which is slightly greater in circumference – encircled in gold.

'A telescope!' she exclaims.

'Close,' Father says.

'Look into it,' Austin suggests.

At first, all she can see are meaningless splotches of colour, then the colours arrange themselves into fragments juxtaposed like translucent jewels. In them she sees the entire Christmas tree, but in pieces, and the pieces topple as she turns the tube, creating images that are both familiar and unfathomable, that reflect and then melt into each other, upending and dividing, as if she had dropped the house on the floor and were frantically trying to glue it back together by turning the shards every which way.

Emily pulls back her eye, dizzy. This instrument takes the world as it is and makes it unrecognizable. While Lavinia unwraps a pretty sewing box, Emily says the most curious thing.

'But I already have so many books…'

'My word, Emily, you can see full well it's not a book,' her mother exclaims.

How can she explain that even though it's not a book, it's not *not* a book either?

Only Austin gets it, and he winks at her. Emily and her brother understand each other without having to spell things out. The first letter he will write using his stationery set will be to Emily – *Dear Lady of the House* – while she walks the rooms, the kaleidoscope pressed to her eye, deconstructing them one by one: the kitchen, the parlour, the dining room, and her bedroom, broken into fragments, her fingers making them spin.

In Emily's bookcase, the books are lined up like soldiers at attention. One contains birds, another shells. Opening a third, she discovers the entire solar system: Mercury, Venus, Earth, Jupiter, Saturn, and Uranus. There are the complete works of Shakespeare. And the Bible, which contains the whole Truth.

Her bedroom holds all that and more, because nothing has been said of the notebooks with their blank pages awaiting everything that doesn't yet exist – the birds, the trees, and the planets that fill her head, her other secret chamber.

Emily attends Amherst Academy, an institution founded by her illustrious grandfather; her father is its treasurer. There is scarcely a venture or a transaction that happens in town without Edward Dickinson's help, and his influence extends beyond state limits, because later he will be elected to the United States Congress. Years earlier, her grandfather sat in the Senate. So it is only natural that Austin should follow in their footsteps, first at the Academy, then at Harvard Law School.

As for the women in the family, Emily Norcross, Emily's mother, is said to have a green thumb. And Lavinia's embroidery is quite pretty. As a little girl, Emily seemed to have inherited her mother's talent and was able to make orchids bloom.

The herbarium Emily Dickinson created as a teenager has been preserved at Harvard University's Houghton Library, where it has been digitized to be viewed online, while the original is safely tucked away from soiled hands.

In sixty-six pages, it features 424 specimens of flowers and plants, arranged with care more aesthetic than scientific. Some entries retain a hint of the colour of the flower picked a century and a half ago. The yellows, in particular, seem not to have been ravaged too badly by the passage of time; the golds have veered toward ochre, the mustards look russet, but the eye instinctively recreates the heart of the daisies. The leaves look like felt, slightly greyed, as if they have been covered in ashes over time.

Reading the flowers as a story, from left to right and top to bottom, we begin with jasmine, one of the two queens of perfumery flowers, long associated with love and desire. Legend has it that Cleopatra sailed to meet Mark Antony on a vessel with sails soaked in essence of jasmine. I like to think that it is not this historical, flamboyant use that gave it its place as the ornamental drop cap of her herbarium, but its other humble, commonplace application: plunged in hot water with tea leaves, its flowers make an exquisite infusion.

The privet comes second. It has white blossoms with a sweet fragrance and poisonous black berries. A dye is extracted from its fruit that long served to blacken rosary beads and to make the violet ink that illuminators prized.

The large jagged leaves of the *Collinsonia canadensis*, or horse balm, sit in the centre of the page. This scented plant, which smells like mint, is used to treat respiratory problems.

It is also one of the medicinal plants that, centuries before Emily made her herbarium – and well before the Puritans' ancestors left their ships to establish their earthly kingdom on the new continent – were used by Indigenous peoples of Massachusetts to heal the first colonists who, during the bitter cold of winter, were dying of scurvy as they lay in the snow. This is a plant that can save your life.

A second spray of jasmine is set at the bottom left, not far from a horseshoe's vetch, the only plant the chalkhill blue – a delicate butterfly with opalescent wings – feeds on.

On the first page of her herbarium, Emily has assembled everything needed by the writer she already is without knowing it, or maybe knowing it: colour to make ink that she can use to write and draw, a source of light, a way to attract butterflies, a balm to heal from the cold, and flowers for tea.

Just like her plants, she will spend the winter between the pages of a book.

In the parlour, Emily and the clock face off, both tall, straight, streamlined. The clock's walnut armour hides its inner workings. Its face is white, and a slender hand sweeps around it. A heavy, golden pendulum swings at knee height. The clock's heart is beating. Emily is dressed in blue. It doesn't suit her complexion, but she doesn't care. All clothes are uncomfortable: her rough linen undergarments, scratchy lace around her neck, velvet so soft it gives her shivers. If she could, she would just go naked, or she would dress in walnut or mahogany. At age thirteen and a few months, she still doesn't know how to tell the time. She adamantly refuses to learn.

Emily doesn't take her eyes off the hand. If she looks away for a second, the monster will devour her. An hourglass is filled with sand, a clepsydra is filled with water, a clock is filled with hours.

Those hours are going to come pouring out all at once: hours of fever, hours wasted awaiting sleep, hours of nightmares, long hours of silence, and the hour of her birth and her death will unfurl in a long tape to strangle her. Emily holds her breath. The hand jumps ahead, and the bells chime, deafening, like a church carillon. The world is saved. Emily skips away, and the clock keeps marking time, which refuses to stand still and which she refuses to tell.

For years, every time we would go to the seaside, I would bring back handfuls of white, rust, mustard yellow, and saffron agate, and pieces of bluish sea glass polished by the waves. Once I was home, I would put them on the bookshelf in my office, between the books. When I pick them up today, it's like the hours spent walking on the beach in the autumn light have crystallized in them, like sap turned to amber. I hold the hours in the palm of my hand.

Sophia Holland, Emily's cousin and best friend, is back from a summer by the sea. With a faint tan, her pale skin is golden, but she has hollow cheeks and beneath her glassy eyes are lilac circles. In her white dress, she is breathtakingly beautiful.

'I've brought you something,' she tells Emily.

'What is it?'

'Guess.'

Emily closes her eyes and holds out her hand. Sophia places in it a flat object, lighter than a pebble, almost perfectly round. With her fingertips, Emily studies its texture – a little rough, like velvet that gets wet and hardens as it dries, and the surface, slightly rounded on one side, is pitted almost imperceptibly.

'I don't know,' Emily says, opening her eyes.

'It's a sand dollar.'

On the rounded side, Emily sees a flower with five petals, or else a star carved in the calcium carbonate. 'Is it a shell?'

'A sea urchin. A flowery urchin with no spines.'

'Is it alive?' Emily presses her ear to the surface to listen for a heartbeat.

'I don't think so. Perhaps.'

'I have something for you, too,' Emily whispers. From her pocket, she pulls a small card folded in half, on which she has glued her most precious possession: a four-leaf clover. 'It's thought to bring good luck.'

Sophia nods her head solemnly.

That night, under her pillow, Emily's fingers touch the sand dollar. She falls asleep dreaming of the land where it is used as currency, of the wonders it could procure: a mockingbird's call, the first snow, a bottomless inkwell, days added to your life.

Brother and sister have maps unfolded in front of them. As they flip the panels, they cross rivers and leap across borders. This is the only type of travel Emily dreams of. Some maps show unfamiliar countries. On other sections, she spots familiar names.

'You see, to get from Amherst to Boston, you have to go through Springfield, Leicester, Worcester, Linden, and Waltham,' Austin explains.

Emily uses her finger to trace the string of towns on the map, saying their names out loud.

'Except,' Austin says, pointing to Linden, 'that one doesn't exist.'

Emily looks at him, perplexed. The name is printed in the same typeface as the others, and maps don't lie.

'It exists only on the map,' Austin explains. 'I know, because I've made the trip twenty times. All that's there is a small stretch of woods and a cornfield. Not even a cabin.'

'But how is that possible?' Emily asks.

'It's a paper town. The people who drew the map invented it to be sure no one would steal their work.'

'Stealing a town, what a strange idea.' Emily says.

'It's not stealing a town, but its name, and its outline,' Austin corrects her. 'If the makers of this map should discover the town of Linden on another map, they will know their work has been copied.'

'A paper town,' Emily repeats.

In her bedroom there is a bed, a chest of drawers, a small table, and a chair, and books piled everywhere. They contain all the countries of the world, all the stars in the sky, the flowers, the trees, the birds, the spiders, and the mushrooms. Multitudes, real and invented. Within the books there are other books, like a house of mirrors, where every mirror reflects another, getting smaller each time, until the people are no larger than mice.

Every book contains one hundred books. They are doors that open and never close. Emily lives in the midst of one hundred thousand drafts. She is always in need of a cardigan.

Nearby, within the onion-skin pages of the Bible, all cities past and present are crammed: Jerusalem, Bethlehem, Sheba, Cana, Sodom and Gomorrah, Capernaum, Jericho, Babylon.

Every time she opens the good book, Emily expects all of these cities and their masses to come gushing out, like in children's books with cut-outs that rise up in complicated folds to form a cabin, a castle, a paper forest.

The golden rays stream like honey through the window. The afternoon light is so thick that Emily feels like a bee caught in amber. Everyone goes about their business in the Dickinson household. Father is preparing for a meeting with an important client; Mother is busy with her migraines; Austin is reviewing his grammar lesson; Lavinia, a cat in her lap, is embroidering a cushion; while, up in her bedroom, Emily is writing a letter to someone who doesn't exist. If she has enough talent, that person will eventually appear.

Words are fragile creatures to pin down on paper. They flutter around the bedroom like butterflies. Or like moths that have escaped from woollens – butterflies lacking colour and a spirit of adventure.

That evening, in a book written by a Frenchman, Emily reads the story of a Jew who lived one hundred lives. One hundred lives, to what end? Not once was he a bird.

Dickinson: son of Dick, Richard, the lionheart.

All of the Jameses, sons of Nathanael, Arthur, Thomas, and Matthew. All of the Johns, Williams, Peters, sons of Joseph, sons of Albert, of Francis, of Samuel, a long male line that just ended with her, she who contains them all.

Where is the suffix for 'daughter of'? Is she of so little importance that there is no point even naming her? Emily, the appleheart.

On the other side of the window, autumn arrives. Fall. The fall of summer, which twirls like helicopter seeds before landing far away, somewhere on the other side of the planet. The leaves in the garden are spinach green, covered with a grey veil the heat of summer has left on them, which looks like the powder that coats some mushrooms. They are getting ready to turn pomegranate red, lemon yellow, orange, while in the tropics where these incredible fruits grow, it is summer year-round. The leaves turn strawberry pink, and fall already holds within it the spring.

The body is laid out on the Hollands' dining room table. It has Sophia's features, her face now just a waxy mask. Emily approaches on tiptoe, as if to avoid waking a sleeping child.

Sophia is dressed in her prettiest dress, pink, with lace cuffs and collar, and her patent leather ankle boots. She has a bow in her carefully curled hair. Emily imagines Mrs. Holland doing her daughter's hair as if she were a doll. People say words stripped of meaning: *typhus, mercy, divine will.*

Sophia doesn't seem serene, or relieved, or asleep. Sophia simply isn't there. She has been replaced by her absence. Emily approaches again, almost close enough to touch her. Tinges of greenish-blue show through the white skin, which is like the surface of lard that has been left out too long in the summer heat. Emily glances over her shoulder. No one is watching her. She reaches into her pinafore, takes out the sand dollar Sophia gave her the year before, and slips it in the pocket of the pink dress, hoping it will be enough.

She doesn't cry, merely clenches her fists in her empty pockets, until she can't feel her fingers. But in the evening, when a ham is brought to the table, glistening with fat under the glare of the lamp, Emily throws up.

The road from home to school isn't that long, but to Emily it feels like she is crossing continents and oceans. The horses' hooves strike the ground with the same rhythm as the thin hand on the grandfather clock that marks the seconds. Father drives in silence. Emily is filled with an emotion she doesn't know, a mixture of fear and impatience that feels like ants crawling up and down her legs and butterflies in her stomach. She is fine with that; it makes for company on the voyage.

The Mount Holyoke Female Seminary is a large, geometric building, four storeys of perfectly aligned windows, four rows high, sixteen windows wide. The top floor, Emily supposes, must be where the students and teachers sleep. Seven chimneys are set on the roof.

'They look like birthday candles, don't they, Father?'

'Hmm?'

'The chimneys.'

He considers them for a moment and then turns back toward this curious child who never says what is expected of her.

'No, in fact,' Emily continues, 'they look more like the smokestacks of a huge ocean liner that has made a stop here, in the middle of the fields.'

'They look like reassurance that you won't freeze in the winter,' Father says, bringing the horses to a halt.

They step down from the carriage, and Edward unloads the large trunk stuffed with Emily's dresses, shawls, petticoats, shoes, books, and kaleidoscope.

Mrs. Lyon comes to greet them. She has deeply lined features on a tired face, an open smile, and eyes that sparkle with intelligence. She addresses Emily first, before greeting her father.

'Welcome, Emily.'

Emily responds with a shallow curtsy. Her father heads to the door, leaving the trunk for someone to get later. But Mrs. Lyon bends down, grabs the leather handle attached to one end and, without further ado, starts to drag it. Seeing her, Emily rushes to grab the other handle. Between them, they manage to lift the trunk a few inches off the ground.

'What on earth?' Edward cries out, alarmed, having finally turned and seen what they were up to.

He hesitates for a moment, not knowing whether it is proper to relieve the slip of a girl or the schoolmistress first. He chooses the latter. She happily relinquishes the handle, gesturing to Emily to do the same.

'I believe I mentioned, Mr. Dickinson, that we do not employ help. The chores are evenly divided among the students and the teachers. This aids in the education of the former and the training of the latter.

But stubborn Emily refuses to put down the trunk, which she ends up carrying, with her father, to the entrance to the seminary, where two teachers have come to help.

Over the years, Father has taught her a great many important things: he has lectured her, instructed her, and educated her, but this is the first time they have actually done *something together*. He wastes no time in leaving, a hand on his aching lower back. Who would have thought mere fabric could be so heavy?

The first apartment we rented in Boston, when my husband's company opened an office in the city a few months after our daughter's birth, was on Holyoke Street. The name seemed strange – at the time, everything seemed strange – but I didn't inquire as to where it came from or what it might mean.

We lived in the South End, the largest Victorian neighbourhood outside of the United Kingdom, occupying the second and third floors of one of the tall red-brick homes typical of the city. From the street, bay windows gleamed like ice in the winter sun. All around the neighbourhood, the sidewalks, made of the same red brick, had been warped over the years by frost and tree roots, rippled as if under the influence of underground waves. The bricks came straight from the holds of ships that docked in the city in the eighteenth and nineteenth centuries; they were used as ballast and, like us, had no doubt crossed half the globe before landing here.

To go outside, we had to go down three flights of stairs, plus an outdoor staircase, as steep as the ladder of a ship and often covered in ice. Just going up to the kitchen (the bedrooms were on the lower floor) required an effort I was reluctant to make; I was afraid of dropping my daughter in the stairway. I have few vivid memories of our time there; I must have spent weeks shut away on the second floor, watching the snow fall outside my window, my little baby in my arms.

Not much happened on Holyoke Street. People bundled up to walk their dogs along the wavy sidewalks in the morning and the evening. The shadows grew longer at the end of the day, and the lights went on in the homes across the street. One afternoon, in the bare branches of a nearby tree I spotted a nest made of twigs and long bits of blue yarn. Spring had arrived.

❧

What does the word *Holyoke* mean? I had neither the slightest idea nor the strength to do the research. By association, I thought of an egg yolk, which I pictured raw, making me feel slightly sick to my stomach. As for Boston, it is the city of Botolph, a seventh-century English saint, the patron saint of travellers. I have never dreamed of travel; I have always sought the opposite: to put down roots, to finally feel at home somewhere. Even though we had no intention of selling the house we had left in Outremont, once we had stepped out the door and turned the key, I felt like it no longer belonged to us. And this apartment would never be our home. We had no home.

The first day, we arrived in the late afternoon after a long car ride, dropped our suitcases in the shadowy light of the apartment, and turned right around to get groceries at Trader Joe's. My daughter was exhausted and irritable, and I wasn't much better. The store was lit with glaring fluorescent lights. I pushed our cart through the endless aisles; it was empty except for a container of hummus. I would have liked to sit down somewhere, anywhere, with my baby, with a hot meal in front of me. I felt like I was going to faint. I said, sulking, 'There's nothing to eat here.'

Then I burst into tears in the middle of the packed grocery store.

A few weeks earlier, someone had asked me, 'Why don't you want to leave your house in Montreal? What do you think you will miss most?'

I thought the point of the exercise was, once those things were identified, to find a way to take them with us, replace them, recreate them, or find an equivalent or substitute.

I gave it a lot of thought before answering.

'The tree I can see from my office window.'

At the seminary, Emily and her classmates study Latin, botany, astronomy, history, mineralogy, literature, and math. One might almost forget they are mere girls.

❧

Books speak of things, of course, and from the pages of thick, dusty volumes that generations before them have held in their hands, the students learn about rocks, stars, and insects. But for Emily, things also speak of books.

One morning, while contemplating the forest, she sees the branches of a tree stir. At first it is gentle, a simple rustling of leaves that could be due to the wind, but soon she is sure of it: the tree has moved. She remembers the fantastic Birnam Wood Shakespeare dreamed up, the army messily coiffed with leaves and branches that begins marching to Dunsinane, armour rattling.

But that is not what Emily sees. In class that week they looked at prints of mangrove swamps; the mangroves with their long roots that emerge from the water like fingers and toes are called *walking trees*. What she sees is an army of maple, pine, ash, and oak trees that slowly extract their roots from the ground and spread them on the earth, feel its solidity, breathe in the air, then slide them a little sideways and forward, like a person with an injured leg learning to walk again. The branches provide a bit of balance, the trunks bend backward just a little, the roots lift from the ground, not very high, then with more conviction. The birds fly from their nests, the chipmunks leap from the ground, creatures are frantic, and this initial silent movement is accompanied by a muffled clamour that can be heard miles around. The forest is running, this very second, it is advancing like a huge wave, a whoosh that won't stop. It will wipe out not only the enemy camp, but also the entire area, Mount Holyoke, where, at her window, eyes shut, Emily waits to be swept away.

But there is nothing to attack, nothing to take or lay siege to, aside from a gaggle of young geese, of which she is one. How much does a goose fetch on the market? It can't be much.

Still, the tree moved, she is sure of it. Standing at her side, Macbeth is uncertain, but the Bard's protagonists are often in doubt – or they take the wrong counsel. What army could swoop down on the seminary this April morning?

The tree moves again; this time it truly starts to walk.

It's a buck, perhaps two years old, its antlers perched high on its head like the crown of a large oak.

Mrs. Lyon cares about more than just filling the minds of the pupils placed in her trust; she also wants to save their souls by leading them to embrace the Lord as she has. But she refuses to terrorize or threaten them to accomplish her goal. She will not convince them to inhabit the kingdom of God with visions of hell. These girls are sensible, educated creatures. She will appeal to their reason and respect their free will. She will leave them at liberty – to say yes.

'Who among you,' she asks in her firm, pleasant voice, 'has already accepted the Lord into her life and her heart?'

Mrs. Lyon has the open face and level gaze of those who have God on their side. The soul at peace, enlightened by certainty.

Most of the young girls raise their hands, some trembling, others with pride. Her eyes scan the room.

'Who among you hopes to do so?'

Most of the remaining girls raise their hands. Mrs. Lyon lets the moment linger.

Finally, she asks, 'Who among you is without hope?'

Six or seven raise their hands. Emily is one of them.

What is this god in three parts: the fearsome Father, the sacrificial Son, the enigmatic Holy Ghost? Why does He refuse to be known? Why does He offer His grace to some and not others? How does one love Him as He should be loved? Feign love? He – They – who is all-seeing, wouldn't He/They figure it out? Isn't that lie worse than the simple observation that

God is a mystery, He is silence, and Emily understands the world first through words? God is an eclipse. He is beyond words. He is not hiding in churches; there is no point looking for Him in the yellowed pages of the King James Bible, of which the Dickinson household has no fewer than eight copies: more good books than souls to save. When Emily looks to the heavens, she sees only clouds. If heaven is rest for the righteous, does that mean they are turned into birds?

In winter, the sun goes down early at Mount Holyoke. The girls eat their dinner by lamplight, while outside the fields are plunged in darkness. Emily's job is to set the cutlery on the tables, and she applies herself to it diligently, as is her habit. She enjoys pointless, repetitive tasks. Every knife, every fork, is an anchor that keeps her on the ground.

The white plates gleam in the lamplight; it is dark blue outside, and the snow is falling in fat flakes, like rabbit fur. The girls are served big bowls of cabbage, potatoes, pieces of lard, turnips, and sliced carrots, which is the regular fare for the week. The girls talk while they eat; they are even encouraged to discuss ideas. Then those whose duty is to clear the table remove the dishes, while the others go up to the common room. There they review their lessons for the next day before getting into their nightgowns.

They quiz each other.

'What is a group of pheasants called?' Anna asks.

'A bouquet,' Isabel says. 'A group of starlings?'

'A murmur.'

'Of flamingos?'

'A flamboyance of flamingos. Of owls?'

Isobel hesitates. Without lifting her eyes from her book, Emily answers for her.

'It is a *parliament of owls*.'

'Well done. Something harder then. What is a group of larks?

'An exaltation.'

'And butterflies?'

'A kaleidoscope of butterflies.'

She observes them, slim waists, white smocks, hair tied back, unalike and yet strangely similar in their youth. And what would you call a group of seminary students, on a winter's eve?

They are all of that at once, of course: exaltation, parliament, flamboyance, kaleidoscope, murmur.

The girls wake up and leap out of bed. They brush their hair one hundred strokes, just like they did before retiring. They dress hastily, choosing their whitest shifts and their prettiest ribbons.

That day, the seminary will receive an almost famous author of a collection of poems, which address mainly Glory, Duty, and the Soul. Many of them have never seen an author in the flesh. Generally, poets are stone statues. The pupils couldn't be more excited than if one of those statues had suddenly come to life.

When the Poet enters the classroom, his hair is pulled back, as if he alone were battling an invisible wind, and he keeps checking the disorder of his untamed hair by running his fingers through it. He is a handsome man, with a high forehead, dark eyes set under arched eyebrows, an aquiline nose, and thin lips, as is fitting for those with lofty thoughts. He makes plenty of gestures when he speaks, some of which are unnecessary.

He looks through the small group of schoolgirls gathered before him, tall young girls, a bit awkward, awed by his presence – which is only natural – who fidget with their fingers and twist the corners of their white pinafores. They are pretty and entirely interchangeable. He is the only one who is unique. Out of the corner of his eye, he spots his reflection in the window and starts speaking mainly for the benefit of his transparent twin.

His clear, deep voice is just a little too loud, as if he were standing on a platform trying to be heard by spectators in the back row of a large room. Emily sighs. She, too, is looking at the window out of the corner of her eye. She is not searching for her reflection but rather for a nest of twigs in which three light blue eggs are resting.

That is where the poetry is, she knows, more than in this man's lofty words. It is hidden under the delicate shell, in the minuscule heart of creatures yet to be born.

And yet, looking at the Poet, handsome as a peacock, she can't help but tremble a little.

In the common room, the girls in white nightgowns, pale as ghosts, take turns considering what they will do when they grow up.

'I will marry the town doctor.'

'I will have three children: two boys and a girl.'

'I will live in a big white house with black shutters.'

'I will read one book a week.'

'I will lie around all day eating shortbreads and drinking lemon tea.'

'I will have a garden that grows nothing but roses.'

'I will cross the sea on an ocean liner.'

'I will play the violin, the piano, and the harp.'

It's Emily's turn. The girls look at her. Under her black hair, she seems even paler than the others, almost translucent; it's as if she is going to take flight or catch fire.

'I will live in Linden.'

At the end of term, Mrs. Lyon polls the souls again. The girls, features drawn from long evenings of study, are excited by the prospect of Christmas. An almost palpable hysteria hangs in the air: final-exam jitters, which smell of vanilla, damp wool, and fresh ink.

'Whoever has welcomed Jesus into their hearts may sit down.'

Dozens of girls settle onto the long benches.

'Whoever hopes to accept him may sit down.'

A second wave. Isobel hesitates at her friend's side. She shoots her a beseeching look, imploring her to join her, or not to be cross with her. But Emily doesn't turn her head or her eyes. Isobel eventually sits, quickly and stiffly, and Emily Dickinson remains standing, all alone. She is the last of the no-hopers.

She would like to feel for the Heavenly Father the fervour that fills the heart when she sees Canada geese flying high overhead, honking, forming and dissolving a V that looks like waves in the ocean. But most of the sermons hold no interest for her, the very idea of God oppresses her at times, terrifies her at others. Her heart is not big enough, her little brain is not deep enough, to accommodate the Mystery, and she ends up telling herself God probably doesn't have much faith in her either.

In front of Emily, rows of silky, neatly coiffed heads are pressed together, prettily accessorized with curls, ribbons, and bows. Heaven will be crowded; they will be stepping on each other's toes in their patent leather ankle boots.

Lacking hope, certainty, or conviction, Emily remains standing, straight as an *i*, filled with possibility.

Hell. Yes, hell will likely be much more peaceful.

Autumn is over, soon it will be Christmas, and I still haven't made the trip to Homestead. I went back to our beach house instead. Every time we walk through the door, I'm astonished that it's still there. One day it will be swept away by the waves. That is what almost happened to the inn that has been standing on the lot next door since the beginning of the last century. Forty years ago, during a particularly violent storm, the wind and the waves caused so much damage that it had to be torn down. No one has been allowed to build on the lot ever since. People say that during the same storm, the sea lifted a neighbour's house and carried it dozens of metres away. The logs used to build the seawall came loose and floated through the streets like the remains of a raft. I quite like the idea that we are spending half the year living in a boat, the anchor of which could break free at any moment.

Every time we go there, I am struck by how much bigger and brighter the sky is than in the city. No doubt it's the proximity of the ocean that gives it ideas. Every time we leave, my heart is broken, and so is my daughter's: she doesn't understand why we don't live year-round with our toes in the water, a sandcastle close by.

Every morning during this time, I visit Emily in a Homestead I have invented from pictures in books and descriptions by witnesses and historians. I enter on tiptoe so I won't tear holes in the paper floors; I don't dare sit down. I leave the door open a crack when I go.

Emily returns to Homestead less than one year after leaving for the seminary. Her parents are concerned about her health; she hasn't been able to shake a respiratory infection. She is happy to go home.

There is so much for a girl to do in Amherst.

Styling her hair, doing and undoing rollers, smoothing curls.

Baking bread.

Collecting eggs from the henhouse; scrambling them for breakfast.

Depending on the day, visiting the poor, the sick, the aged, women recovering from childbirth, the destitute, the bedridden, and friends, of course, who number in the dozens.

Buying three buttons, a pound of sugar, a yard of lace, black shoelaces, a white petticoat, cinnamon, flint, silk remnants, a bottle of purple ink.

Embroidering a dozen hankies.

Preparing large baskets of fried chicken, cucumber, and fresh bread, filling a bottle with lemonade, cutting watermelon, folding a tablecloth over it all, remembering to tuck in forks, knives, and linen napkins, for a picnic.

Receiving a merchant, a friend, an acquaintance, a passing visitor, a beggar who beats a path to the door; buying from the first, welcoming the second, greeting the third, offering the fourth something to drink, slamming the door in the face of the fifth.

Putting the last of the raspberries on the stove, with their weight in sugar. Simmering. Sterilizing the jars with boiling water. Pouring the jam in the jars and sealing until winter.

Helping Mother lard the roast and peel the vegetables, setting the table, clearing the table, drying the dishes, putting them away, setting the glasses upside down on the rim.

Attending an outdoor concert with all the young people in town.

Only once Emily closes her bedroom door behind her and steps into the silence can she start to hear the voice that speaks, and yet doesn't, deep in her head.

The leaves have fallen from the trees in the garden. All except one, a young maple, at the back of the yard, which has kept its yellow mane, where the sunbeams come to warm themselves. It is a small fire burning, dancing in the wind, defying the approaching cold, indifferent to the silent omen of the other trees whose bare branches are like charred embers. The crows keep their distance, so nothing disrupts its golden splendour. The maple hangs its lanterns in mid-air. Who needs stained glass in a church when there is a tree like this in the garden?

It stays very much alive until winter, when the others have fallen into the deep sleep of plants. Its leaves keep making the stars shine through the long December nights.

Since she was a child, she has been able to spot Orion, with its sleek hourglass figure, the dog leading the way. She long ago decided it would be her next home.

The Bible is filled with unfathomable mysteries. The human spirit is weak, but there is one thing Emily understands perfectly: Eden was first a garden.

Winter passes like a dream.

Austin, Emily, and Lavinia, trailing three flickering shadows, walk together through the tree-lined paths where invisible birds sing. The perfume of white flowers, apples, plums, and strawberries floats in the air. The weather is deliciously mild. The grass is greener here than it is anywhere else, almost emerald.

Sophia's grave is one of the freshest in the cemetery. They stand before it and bow their heads. Emily kneels and places her hands on the warm stone.

Sophia is not the youngest person in the cemetery, far from it. Dozens of babies are buried here, little girls and boys resting under the ground in their Sunday best, dead from consumption, the flu, the measles, anemia, croup, fright, rage, boredom. Their pale ghosts, concealed by the trees in bloom, play tag. They hide behind the spindly wooden crosses, spreading their arms in imitation; they run as fast as their diaphanous legs will carry them down the pathways, laughing in silence.

Without a word, Austin and Lavinia start walking again. They have other dead to visit. It was a hard winter. Emily remains kneeling for a long time on her friend's grave. She would like to talk to her, but the grass is deaf and mute. When Emily finally stands, her shadow remains lying on the ground. When it in turn rises, rather than following her, it heads off to race with the little ghosts.

Emily keeps her baby teeth, twenty baroque pearls in an inlaid box on her desk. Some nights, she tells herself that the little girl they belonged to will return for them, a toothless little ghost.

❧

She is too tall, her neck too long, her legs too stiff. She should have been born a scarecrow in a field, surrounded by the starlings and the pumpkins. She would have spent a lazy summer with them, drenched by rain showers, watching the squash swell in the sun. And then, at harvest time, she, too, would be picked and thrown on the fire. What a flambé she would have made, with her dry arms, her stiff legs, her long hair, her matchstick heart.

In the morning, when she awakens, Emily discovers a red flower on her sheet. The same stain is on her nightgown and her cotton drawers.

Mother finds her in the kitchen, bent over the washtub, frantically scrubbing the sheet in the soapy water.

'What on earth are you doing? It's not Monday!'

'I'm sick,' Emily says, in an even tone. 'I'm bleeding. I'm probably going to die.'

'Oh, is that all it is,' her mother answers, disgust and discomfort vying in her voice. 'You're not sick. You've become a woman. It happens to all of us.'

Emily stops scrubbing. So all women are sick. That explains certain things – why it is that men exercise the occupations of attorney, doctor, notary, and pastor. The sheet expands in the washtub like a sea creature, a jellyfish or anemone in the pink water. She can't feel her fingertips.

'It happens once a month,' Mother goes on, 'and it lasts a few days.'

So be it, Emily thinks, as she resumes her scrubbing with renewed rage. A few days a month I will be a woman. The rest of the time I will write.

With Austin off studying at Harvard, every day Emily writes him letters, trying to make them lively, light, and irresistible, in the hopes that he will come home. But he doesn't come home. Her letters are not doing the trick. She needs to send him butterflies.

At the dinner table, her beloved brother's chair is empty. His absence is a hole in Emily's chest. Father is wearing his expression reserved for dark days. It must have been a bad day at the firm. He is beset by *important* concerns, the worries of a man who goes into town, meets other men, and together they solemnly decide on the fate of the world, with its women, children, dogs, cats, and all the other lesser creatures.

Mother looks absent, as she increasingly does. She brings the fork to her mouth mechanically, like an automaton. Her eyes are glass beads. Lavinia drops small pieces of chicken on the floor that are snatched up by a fat ginger cat she recently adopted that rubs against her legs, purring.

Stunned, Emily watches these strangers that life has given her as family. Why wasn't she born to a nest of robins? At least she would have learned the essentials: singing, flying, building a nest.

The second year in Boston, the apartment we rented occupied the second, third, and fourth floors of another tall Victorian home, which was renovated from basement to attic with typical American ostentation: a large granite island in the kitchen, gold chandeliers, expensive faucets in rather poor taste. But the rooms were pleasant and bright, and my mother had a floor to herself when she came to visit.

My daughter and I had gone back to Montreal, so my husband had to furnish the apartment on his own. He went to Ikea where he bought, roughly, one or more of everything, as if filling an empty dollhouse: a table, four chairs, a crib, a changing table, two beds, two mattresses, sheets, pillows, comforters, towels, three chests of drawers, a wardrobe, four bedside tables, lamps, a coffee table, a footstool, dishes, linens and dusters, a coffee maker, a teapot, a vegetable peeler, scissors, cutlery, a can opener, a whisk, two cutting boards, a set of pots, a set of frying pans, a corkscrew, a kettle, a garbage can, three trash cans, a sofa, cushions, three carpets, a dish rack, a broom and a bucket, brushes, sponges...

He had to make a half-dozen trips, each time pushing two overflowing carts, and the bill, of which I prefer not to know the final tally, was a sundry inventory that was not unlike the dizzying lists in *Life: A User's Manual.*

We arrived during a cold snap, and the temperature in the house was around ten degrees. The owner, who was spending the winter in Florida, had forgotten to have the storm windows put in. We took refuge at a hotel until they were installed. From the fourth floor of the Fairmont, where we occupied three rooms overlooking the street, we could see the square in front of the church, where two years later bombs would explode, killing three marathon runners.

At the time, the almost supernatural quiet of frigid weather reigned. There was virtually no one outdoors. The few passersby scurried, chins tucked into their scarves. On television they talked about record low temperatures, unusual precipitation (some ten centimetres of snow had fallen, nothing to get excited about in Montreal, but Boston wasn't equipped for that sort of accumulation), and absurd images played in a loop of a snowplow that had caught fire in the middle of a major artery. Through the frosted windows of our rooms, Copley Square looked like the Kremlin.

We went back to the apartment once the storm windows had been installed, but the temperature had risen four or five degrees at best. When we lifted the wooden radiator covers, we discovered that the cast-iron radiators had been removed during the renovations. Apparently, the skinny hot-water pipes running along the walls were supposed to heat the three storeys on their own – not to mention that the furnace, which was not up to the task, would periodically overheat and shut down completely.

Shivering, a hat on my head and boots on my feet in this ostentatiously luxurious apartment, I remember looking, incredulously, at the long, empty boxes where the radiators should have been. The people who had gilded everything and added skylights had *removed the heating*.

With the apartment furnished, the desperately bare walls remained. Online I ordered reproductions of old botanical prints (*Brassica, Beta vulgaris, Carota*) to hang in the kitchen and the dining room, and a few colourful posters, including an ostrich head – most dignified, with pearls around its neck, and a Picasso with a complicated composition, which I didn't pay much attention to until two-year-old Zoé pointed out to me solemnly, 'The painter drew himself,' and I saw that it was in fact a self-portrait in front of an easel. It nearly did the trick. You could almost have believed people lived here.

From Montreal, we also brought a huge poster from the Peter Doig exhibition at the Museum of Fine Arts, entitled *No Foreign Lands*, which seemed to be a sort of promise, or program. Plus, I felt like I was thumbing my nose at the city by plastering the large letters of the word *Montréal* on the wall of this Boston apartment. But the poster measured almost two metres square, and the blue putty I used to stick it to the plaster wasn't sticky enough to keep it stuck. The poster came down every night while we slept, and every morning I would find it rolled up on the floor in front of the sofa.

One afternoon, my mother and I went out for a walk with my daughter, who was bundled up in her stroller. On Tremont Street, we walked by wine shops and fine grocery stores and fashionable restaurants and bars. I was looking at the windows, feeling firmly on the *outside*, in more ways than I could have explained. Then, through a partially open door, I spotted a series of small pictures hung on a brick wall.

They weren't exactly prints or collages, but pages taken from old books, on which the artist had sketched in black ink signs that looked like characters from a forgotten alphabet. The one I was drawn to showed a large sphere on top of a string of minuscule calculations. I climbed the stairs to ask the price.

The owner said she would sell me the picture, but only once the exhibition was over. She asked for my phone number. I didn't have one. We agreed I would go back in ten days. Before leaving, I bought a terribly expensive old brass cricket with one antenna drooping a little. Turning it between my fingers, I kept saying *crickets on the hearth,* and thinking about the Chinese who, in storybooks, kept insects in little wooden cages.

When we left that apartment one year later to return to Outremont for good, the cricket and the print were wrapped in boxes with the rest of our things and left in storage. I can barely remember the composition, even less the title of the piece – *True North,* perhaps? In any event, it was something to do with staying the course.

If you ask Emily to draw a young girl, she will draw a portrait of Susan: pretty, lively, proud, and intelligent. She is what Emily would like to see when she looks in the mirror, a sort of ideal twin. The two friends are as thick as thieves. Together they wander the familiar streets of Amherst, pick flowers from gardens, can jam, and tell each other fanciful stories.

Susan has porcelain skin, a round red mouth like a cherry, and wild curls that dance around her cheeks. Emily holds back from gently touching and rearranging the curls, as she would with a doll.

One afternoon when Sue comes to visit Emily, it is Austin, freshly back from Harvard, who answers the door. He has known her since she was a child, but now, in his absence, she has grown into an adult. He is a few years older, and he already knows how to seem like a man.

'Well, hello,' Austin says, searching desperately for something to add.

'I didn't realize you were home,' Susan says. 'Did you enjoy Boston?'

She lowers her eyes, looking up at him from beneath her lashes.

'It's a fine city, but Amherst holds certain attractions it doesn't.'

This is said with a penetrating look that makes the young girl blush.

When Emily comes downstairs, Susan is sitting in the parlour, and Austin is reading to her. She is now his guest. Soon she will be shared equally between brother and sister.

❧

When she sees them together, something clenches in her chest like a fist.

Her heart is black; it harbours a feeling that consumes her. Emily is jealous, and twice over: of the love Austin has for Susan, and of the love Susan feels for Austin in return. She would like these two loves to be lavished on her. She feels doubly, even triply, cheated, because she is betrayed by her own heart as well. Her heart is a hunk of coal that has been burned twice, which is to say, a heap of ashes.

On the mantelpiece, the invitations and death notices for the year line up like garland, both light and dark. One by one, her friends are being snatched by marriage or malady. In one year, Emily has attended so many weddings and so many funerals that she has a hard time distinguishing in her mind all the farewell ceremonies in which young girls seem disguised, no longer quite themselves.

The dead are seen only in dreams. As for the girls who marry, some are already growing thicker at the waist, their gestures more listless, walking with their feet turned out, as if they were clutching an egg between their legs. Soon they will go nowhere without a screaming little pink creature in their arms. Soon they will no longer belong to themselves at all. Emily shivers at the thought. She turns to Lavinia, who is sewing near the window with a cat in her lap, and asks, 'Between the two evils of love and death, which would you choose?'

Lavinia shrugs. She has an *understanding* with a local young man that satisfies her completely and that she does not feel the need to discuss. She rises, saying, 'I'm going to make us some tea.'

In the garden, the first leaves are already wilting.

The two sisters are wearing their best dresses. They have done their hair in front of their mirrors, paying particular attention to their curls and ribbons. Lavinia pinches her cheeks and bites her lips to make the blood flow to them. Emily is as pale as snow. They sit side by side on a white wood church pew.

The bride advances, timidly. She is not used to being the centre of attention. The groom isn't doing much better, but he forces himself to put on a brave front. They have seen each other perhaps twenty times before this day; they have written each other exquisitely polite letters, paid uneasy visits. They are both twenty-one years old. He is an attorney; she is a woman, so she will be an attorney's wife. And a mother, of course. Emily sees the bride's fate laid out before her, plotted out in advance, a shadow cast.

There is always something to do at Homestead: hulling strawberries, polishing the silver that grows tarnished in the cabinets as soon as you turn your back, adding a few pieces to a quilt for a baby yet to be born, sorting clothes to send to the poor, paying suppliers, following the flight of a bee in the garden – but that, that is the work of a lifetime.

Emily is in the kitchen making bread. Under her fingers, the dough is soft, warm, and elastic, like familiar skin. She kneads in long strokes, front to back, repeated one hundred times. After the sixty-second time pressing her palms to the table, she stops, looks around her, grabs the empty bag of flour and tears a piece from it. She takes out a stub of a pencil from her pocket, jots down a few words – sixteen, to be exact, and five dashes as long as sighs – then she folds the piece of paper up tightly, until it takes no more room than a fingernail in the pocket of her apron. She goes back to kneading the bread. Sixty-three.

In a desk drawer, she keeps the poems hastily scribbled on packaging. When she takes them out again, she recognizes them by smell: some have the whiff of flour, others the scent of pepper or pecans. Her favourite smells of chocolate.

To take a stroll one hundred times, one thousand times, more bountiful than the day before, one has only to stroll every day in the same garden.

One day, Emily spotted under a pile of leaves a family of hedgehogs comically curled up together – their spines pointing outward, as they should be.

Another time, right in front of her eyes, a robin pulled out of the ground a worm so long that it broke. The bird ate half of it, and the other part carried on with its half life.

One spring afternoon, it was raining so hard that drops hit the ground and rebounded like nails, and it looked like the rain was rising up from below.

For months, she had strolled in the company of Sophia, whose laughter rose and continued to rise, near the apple trees, in front of clumps of zinnias.

One day in November, the first snow started to fall just as she lifted her head toward the sky, astonished – the first snow is the first every time.

Early one morning, she came upon a magpie with a gold bracelet in its beak.

These days are overlaid like sheets of tracing paper to form a single image made of one hundred layers: hedgehogs, robin, magpie, and snow now accompany them on their strolls, her and the memory of Sophia.

While Emily walks in the garden, Mother slips into her bedroom, the door of which is always shut. Everything is in order, the quilt smoothed over sheets drawn tight, the pillow with no creases: it is like the cell of a cloistered nun.

Mother opens the drawers and searches for something, not knowing what. She has never been nosy, a serious flaw; it is her sense of duty, of course, that has propelled her into her daughter's sanctuary – she is doing it reluctantly, unwillingly.

In a drawer of the small desk is a bundle of papers covered with Emily's fine handwriting, which a teacher at Mount Holyoke compared to the tracks made by the feet of prehistoric birds, preserved in the school's museum, a comparison that had made Edward Dickinson furrow his brow and that slightly alarmed his wife. What was this child who had gotten it in her head to write like a bird, and a dead one at that?

She picks up the first piece of paper, part of a hastily torn sheet, and turns it over. On one side, she can make out Emily's gingerbread recipe – isn't this the one that the summer before had won her daughter the town's annual baking contest? On the other side is a string of words that bear no real relationship to each other. The text is curiously broken up with long dashes. Some sort of list?

I reckon — When I count at all —
First — Poets — Then the Sun
Then Summer — Then the Heaven of God
And then — the List is done —

She reads it again, perplexed, a strange incantation, then carefully sets down the piece of paper, on the gingerbread side, before tiptoeing out.

1 quart flour
½ cup butter
½ cup cream
1 tablespoon ginger
1 teaspoon soda
1 teaspoon salt
Make up with molasses

Austin and Susan have their house built on the property next to Homestead, a stone's throw from the grand home. The neighbours knock on each other's doors a dozen times a day to borrow a book, share an article, bring over a pie that is still warm, return a magnifying glass, check a recipe, bring back a print, ask for information, deliver news, leave sheet music. A path runs from Homestead to Evergreens. It, too, is in a rush.

❧

Emily watches them through the windows of the parlour and the dining room, where they are outlined like a life-sized Chinese shadow play. She follows them to the bedroom, and then she turns her back. She doesn't like to imagine them between the rumpled sheets. She prefers, in her mind, to place the puppets in their box where they lie sensibly like flowers set out to dry.

The garden is larger than the sum of all the galaxies, which cannot possibly contain so many ants, flowers, and blades of grass. It is the entire universe, bounded to the south by the main road, to the east by the hemlock bush, to the west by Evergreens, and to the north by generations of Dickinsons born onto and buried under this land. The first, Nathaniel, arrived in 1630 along with John Winthrop and some seven hundred other Puritans. The fleet had eleven ships, and history has not retained the name of the ship aboard which great-grandfather Dickinson made the voyage: the *Arabella,* the *Talbot,* the *Ambrose,* the *Jewel,* the *Mayflower* (not the famous *Mayflower* – another one), the *Whale,* the *Success,* the *Charles,* the *William and Francis,* the *Hopewell,* or the *Trial.* No document attests to it, but Emily knows: leaving whale, jewel, trial, and hope to others, her ancestor definitely crossed the ocean in the hull of a flower.

Monday, laundry day. Emily takes in the clean washing from the clothesline and folds it, making piles for household linens, for Mother's, Lavinia's, or her own clothing and undergarments.

Suddenly, she hears a sigh.

Mother is standing in the doorway, looking tired, as always. She shakes her head.

'My dear girl, I have told you a hundred times, that is not how you fold a petticoat.'

Emily looks up. It's true. She has been told a hundred times. A hundred times she hasn't listened. So how do you do it? She doesn't know. If Mother says it a hundred and one times, she still won't listen.

'What a sorry homemaker you would have been, my child. It's probably best that you remained a spinster.'

'You're right. Some women aren't cut out to be mothers.'

Mother leaves, shuffling her feet, her slippers scuffing along the floor like sandpaper. Emily looks at the piles of clothes before her, resists the temptation to rumple Mother's clothes and tread on them. Instead, she lifts one of her own shifts, pearl grey, wads it into a ball, and throws it on the ground. She does the same with her pink handkerchiefs, her ecru chemises, a burgundy skirt, and a blue petticoat, keeping only the pristine white clothes, which she takes upstairs to put in her drawers. The colours stay on the ground, vanquished, defeated.

In a dream, she takes her clothes by the armful and throws them out the window into the middle of the yard, where they form a mountain of brown, green, grey, midnight blue, and purple. The stockings wrap around the petticoats like boas. The dresses lie there, writhing. The skirts open like fans. The pile contains woollens, cottons, linen, and scratchy mourning lace. Once it's all there, she takes out a match and strikes it, holds it for a moment before her eyes and throws it on the pile, which goes straight up in flames. Nothing burns faster than things that have been abandoned.

Emily stretches out her hands in front of the pyre to warm her fingers. In the smoke rising to the sky, she can make out the stiff silhouette of an almost new dress and a wool jacket that kept her warm the winter before.

Sophia awaits them, perched on a cloud. She hasn't aged. With the sprightliness of a fifteen-year-old, she slips on the dress, puts on the jacket, and sashays about, imitating the way a lady would walk. The little ghost in her Sunday best bursts out laughing, while, in the yard, anything that is not white continues to burn.

That is what Emily dreams. But in real life, she gently takes the clothing she will wear no more, folds the items with as much care as if she were putting them away for the season, then piles them in crates that Lavinia will distribute during her next round of good works. The poor can never have too much colour.

In the heat of the hearth, where a large cast-iron pot is hanging, Lavinia measures, weighs, pours, grates, peels, seeds, hulls, clips, pares, mixes, infuses, slices, sprinkles, tosses, seasons, sweetens, glazes, spices, cinnamons, gingers, nutmegs, dices, soaks, tempers, sifts, bastes, whips, beats, crushes, grinds, oils, braises, shells, stems, hulls, steeps, marinates, kneads, shapes, lines, brushes, coats, tops, flours, carves, prunes, thins, hashes, dilutes, trims, husks, scales, shucks, cuts, chops, lards, fills, trusses, slivers, moulds, flips, scrapes, pods, roasts, sautés, browns, mashes, grills, poaches, fries, simmers. She has never dreamed of being a magician. What is the point, when you can be a witch?

Lavinia knits mufflers and scarves; she embroiders hankies, mends skirts, sews aprons. Emily does the opposite. As her sister dresses them, Emily undresses in the silence of her bedroom. First, she removes popular beliefs and manners, and then God and His cortège, visits, obligations, and smiles. Soon, all that will remain is for her to slip out of her skin and stand in front of the mirror, all teeth and pointy ribs, a tiny skeleton, white as snow.

In Boston, all of the city's residents looked like close or distant cousins of John F. Kennedy: the same forthright stare, the same smile, the same studied casual air. They all seemed to be recent Harvard graduates, and I could swear they had all spent the weekend on the Cape, playing ball with gaggles of children and having clambakes on the beach. In the stores and in the streets, all of these Kennedys were charming, uniformly smiling and eager, astonishingly affable to a Montrealer like me. What hid behind it I will never know. For me, Boston remained a paper town.

❧

One blue evening in spring, as the sun set, we went past the ballet school just as its large doors opened. A cloud of swanlike little girls, buns perched high on their heads, came out and tore down the steps, laughing. There had been auditions that day for the role of Clara in *The Nutcracker*. Outside on the sidewalks and in the street, their equally slender mothers were waiting, with their flawless hair, ankle boots, and big coats, a large scarf wrapped around their necks, beautifully elegant on a late Sunday afternoon (how Boston women manage to be beautifully elegant at any time of day, under any circumstance, escapes me). One by one, they opened their arms. All of them, down to the last one, had landed the role of mother of the ballerina.

❧

At the time, we were looking for a house on the water not too far from the city that was to be our new home. We immediately dismissed the Cape: too expensive, crawling with people, invaded by tourists in the summer and by Bostonians on even the most insignificant long weekend. We had been spending our summers at Cape Elizabeth in Maine for a few years, on a huge property that had fields, forests, two tiny cemeteries, a pond, dunes, nineteen-century buildings falling prettily into ruins, stables for purebreds, a landing strip where a handful of colourful Cessnas set down, an orchard, a small farm where striped Galloway cattle were raised, and I don't know what else. This was all set on dozens of square kilometres, the size of a nature reserve, and that is just what it was, in a way, because from the windows of the house we rented we would regularly spot deer, families of turkeys or guinea fowl, rabbits, eagles, and even, sometimes, at a bend in the path, a porcupine the size of a Labrador. The property also had a beach with sand so white it seemed almost lunar, as soft as flour, a deserted beach we got to along a winding path that crossed a marsh, pine woods, and dunes, like little fairy-tale kingdoms.

This is what I saw in my mind's eye as we left that morning, toward what in Boston is known as the North Shore, having decided to head north along the coast until we found a seashore that would welcome us. The day was grey and cold for spring; the trees still didn't have leaves. It could have been November. We had driven for about thirty minutes to leave the city via Route 1, where a ribbon of big-box stores, theme restaurants, gas stations, and parking lots runs for kilometres, and where, from a distance, the locked cars bring to mind insects with shells that gleam in the sun.

We kept heading north. Stores eventually gave way to bedroom communities, which gave way to yet more bedroom communities, in a seemingly endless succession. It is not out of some affectation that I use this term rather than *suburb*; the fragmentation implicit in the expression conveys the atmosphere of this waterfront, where, on the other side of the highway, cube apartment buildings stood, along with houses probably built in the 1950s with no regard for architecture or urban planning. It was as if someone, using a huge saw, had cut off a slice of a small, soulless industrial town and transplanted it here, near the waves.

We got out of the car. There was no one, anywhere, no passersby, no one walking, not even a bird. The wind whipped our faces. The smell of salt, bleak and mineral, floated in the air. The ocean stretched before us in short, choppy waves, flint grey. It wasn't really the sea.

Emily of the fields has never been to the sea. The moving blue expanse scares her. She is completely at ease in the prism that a drop of water, just one, traces on her bedroom window. When she dreams of the ocean, she is afraid of falling into it like you would plummet to the foot of a cliff. There are risks to flirting with the infinite.

People said she started by not going into town as much, then she stayed confined to the garden, and then barely left the house, then the second floor, finally taking up residence in her bedroom, which she would leave only when strictly necessary. But in reality, she had long been living in a space much smaller: a piece of paper the size of her palm.

No one could take that home away from her.

❧

All she needs is to lay down a few sentences, sometimes just a few words, on paper to feel soothed, for a moment delivered from this nameless, pointless urgency that consumes her. Even saved. What is the catastrophe from which she tries to rip these lines? Oblivion, death, the inferno of the world? She couldn't say.

While the country is tearing itself apart in civil war, Emily is coming undone too, stitch by stitch. She doesn't know what to think about this wholesale carnage, and the God that watches over it, the burned houses and plantations, the maimed, the fields where young men sleep, as handsome as dolls.

The country is no longer hers. It has stopped being hers; it is trying to blow itself up, and her heart, her poor heart, the locus of the turmoil, slowly rips open every evening and is somehow mended in the morning. Now she knows it was not Prometheus's liver that the eagle came to feed on every day.

❧

When her day is almost at an end, Emily goes out into the garden. The last rays come to lie down among the leaves, in a great jumble of brass, as if the instruments in a silent orchestra were lying strewn on the ground, left by the musicians. Somewhere not far off, someone is making a fire of branches, and the smoke winds in a thin yellowish wisp between the garden squash, pot-bellied like orange, apricot, and butter wineskins. Geese fly overhead, piercing the silence with their honking, noisily squawking their route, then calm slowly closes back around everything, like a wound healing.

At this very moment, standing in the middle of autumn, Emily is at the crossroads of two eternities – the summer that is no more and the winter yet to come. She has to stand still, head held high, to avoid slipping into either one, to continue stepping cautiously along the edge of a blade of grass.

One hundred years after Emily Dickinson's death, a Montreal poet noted:

> *Poetry is just the evidence of a life. If your life is burning well, poetry is just the ash. Sometimes you confuse yourself and try to create ashes instead of fire.*

In discovering the sign or the trace of a thing, it is tempting to try to recreate the sign rather than the thing itself, and, in so doing, to sacrifice the quarry for the shadow. Running after the signs of success – but what are they? I am certain Emily Dickinson never tried to create ashes. Fire? Perhaps. I think instead that flames rose up behind her after she passed, without her noticing, busy as she was watering her flowers.

The girls from Mount Holyoke have grown into women. Most of them are married, almost all of those married are mothers. From what Emily can see, none of their young girls' dreams have come true, those they announced while they sat in a circle in their white nightgowns, their whole lives ahead of them. None of them, except hers.

She has long been living in her paper house. One cannot have both a life and books – unless one chooses books once and for all and records one's life in them.

Emily does not for one moment envy the respectable citizens who look after their husband's career, the design of the nursery, the youngest who is slow to start walking. What she wonders is where all the girls from that evening have gone, where have their dreams gone? How can they have changed so much and still answer to the same name?

Suddenly it occurs to her that the girls are still at Mount Holyoke. If she pushed open the door to the dormitory, she would find them, sitting in a circle, their eyes shining in the golden halo of the lamp.

We continue to inhabit the places we have lived long after we leave them. Walking past the apartment where a friend lived with her family, I can still hear the children's cries. Every time I walk along rue de Souvenir, I have to stop myself from going to ring the bell of the unit on the second floor where my husband and I lived during our first five years together, with Fido the tabby, Vendredi the Siamese, and Victor the Great Dane. Part of me is convinced that it will be a twenty-five-year-old Fred, with a rounder face and hair with no grey, who would answer the door. Another version of us continues to live with Victor the dog in a cottage at Inn by the Sea, in Cape Elizabeth. At this very moment, he is lying on the rug there, his muzzle between his enormous paws. He is waiting for us. These versions of us in different places exist all at the same time.

Emily spent her early childhood and her adult life at Homestead, the name of which suggests that it was the very incarnation of what is home – more than a house, a hearth; more than a hearth, the fire that burns in it. And how is it that in French, with *maison,* we don't have a better word to describe what is not the place we inhabit but the place where we live – more than a place, the very life beating inside it?

At this point in time, there are still plenty of visitors to Homestead and Evergreens. The home attracts the cream of society from Amherst and beyond: attorneys, affluent businessmen, pastors, even editors, who come to play the piano, sing, and merrily chat.

On his own, Samuel Bowles would have been a man like any other – if the others were also owners of a prominent newspaper like the *Springfield Republican*. But it wasn't the newspaper that gave him his standing; it was being Mary's husband. Similarly, her standing was based on being her brilliant husband's wife. They soon become regular visitors to the two homes. Emily, as she does with those she loves and by whom she would like to be loved, soon begins sending them letters that are lively, tender, and wild, like puppies.

In writing to either of them (or to one with the other in the wings), Emily writes to a single, hybrid creature, both actor and witness, doubly familiar to her, as she is constantly split in two, trying to live and write life at the same time.

Husband and wife appear elevated, made sublime by the other's gaze, which acts like a magnifying prism. The presence of this third point in the epistolary conversations is kind of reassuring, like a guardrail that lets you approach the abyss without fear of falling in. This phantom recipient is the real recipient of most of the letters Emily feverishly writes, by lamplight, striving to be sufficiently spiritual for two, trying to charm one through the other. It is both twice and half a love.

Wherever she goes, Lavinia is trailed by a herd of cats. On this morning, there are three: a large orange-and-white tomcat, a young black cat that Emily is seeing for the first time, and a female tabby whose swollen belly suggests that she will soon give birth to a litter.

In the kitchen, there is always a saucer of cold milk the neighbourhood cats come to drink from, after which they rub up against her skirts. One could swear she purrs in contentment with them. Carlo, Emily's dog, likes to lap up the milk with a single swipe of his tongue, as kittens look on, scandalized by his bad manners.

The dog sleeps at the foot of her bed. From time to time, his whiskers twitch. In a dream, he is chasing horrifying creatures. Emily places her icy feet against his warm flank; she sinks her toes into the thick fur. Why on earth would she need a husband?

Lavinia sleeps surrounded by her tomcats, large and small. She doesn't have a favourite. She loves the gentle idea of *cat* in each of them, in a thousand variations.

In the copper bathtub, her hair floats in clumps of black seaweed. Her skinny arms and legs are long white eels. She sinks imperceptibly under the warm water, one millimetre at a time, until her face is covered with a transparent layer that looks like ice. She keeps her eyes open.

Over forty, she is barren, as is said about unproductive land, fish that don't lay eggs, and all of the things that, having no other lives than their own, will not survive their own death. *Barren*, like *bare*, naked, with her sagging breasts, empty little pockets veined in blue, her stomach with its skin loose despite never having carried anything, contained anything, enveloped anything, her legs and sex that have long received no caress other than that of the sheets while she sleeps.

The barren woman is naked, as stripped and lacking as a tree in winter. Emily is no fool. Her poems aren't paper children. They are, at best, snowflakes.

Time does not pass; it stands still. Every day lasts an eternity, an entire life in the hours between sunrise and sunset. Every night is a little death. Yet she awakens the next day, astonished to be there. She has been given another chance, but to do what?

She gets up, goes to the window. It's cloudy. A fine rain is falling, leaving a shiny film on the leaves. Mist rises from the garden, and the trees are outlined in ghostly silhouettes. She shivers, draws her shawl around her shoulders, lights the fire that has gone out in the night. The wood crackles, the sparks fly up the chimney. Without thinking, she opens her desk drawer, takes out a piece of paper that she brings to her nose. The poem smells like cloves.

She needs so little that she could just as well be dead – or have never even existed.

As she writes, she erases herself. She disappears behind the blade of grass that, if not for her, we would never have seen. She does not write to *express* herself, perish the thought. The word makes her think of *expectorate,* and in either case the result can be only sticky phlegm, full of mucus; she doesn't write to be noticed. She writes to bear witness: here lived a flower, for three days in July, the year of 18**, killed by a morning shower. Each poem is a tiny tomb erected to the memory of the invisible.

She is flesh, blood, and ink. Ink flows through her veins; the words she writes are raspberry red, drawn from the fine blue lines that quiver under her skin.

She thinks of the poet who visited Mount Holyoke, who explained wanting to put down on the page the emotions that inhabited him, being loathsomely convinced that his inner landscape was so interesting that he invited others to take a stroll through it to contemplate its flower beds and mountain ranges.

He was not only incapable of true poetry but, happy innocent that he was, he was incapable of seeing he was incapable, like someone who is deaf from birth and, having seen someone finger the keys on a piano, composes a sonata by randomly pressing the black and white keys in a pattern that is pleasing to the eye. He will never know what he doesn't know.

Yet this man had ideas; you could see it right away, and they were more important to him than anything.

He nourished them, catalogued them, cultivated them, breathed in their perfume, and urged others to do the same. Emily writes about the world she inhabits, knowing that it would be more beautiful still if it were uninhabited.

Author, from the Latin *augere,* to increase. The author adds. On the other side of the window, the flower garden that grows outdoors echoes the paper garden Emily cultivates through the winter.

Seated at her table in front of her window, she transcribes the faded garden she alone can still see under the snow, a text half erased that she squints to decipher before it disappears altogether. The sun sets early. Starting at three o'clock, the shadows lie down on the ground to sleep, the grounds are a forest stretched out, flattened between the pages of a giant herbarium. She continues to dip her pen in the inkwell even though she can no longer make out silhouettes either inside or out.

The smell of soup and the clinking of cutlery rise from the kitchen. Even in the midst of all of this white, you need to eat. From the imagined lilies and zinnias, a contingent of fuzzy turnips and a battalion of yellow potatoes burst through, led by a cabbage that has lost part of its head. It doesn't take any more than that for the paper garden to start growing, untamed, overrun with wild grasses, dishevelled, which Emily uses to make wreaths rather than scratching them out.

To write, *scribere,* digging in the earth, exhuming, scratching out. She looks up at the trees outside and can't see them anymore. In the dark, the window has become a mirror.

Author, *auctor,* also means God, a word she doesn't know the meaning of. Who needs God when there are bees?

How do others attend to their affairs, big or small, or hold jobs, sew dresses, have children, go on picnics? How do they tear themselves away from the rapture that takes her over when she looks out the window? Don't their eyes see the same thing as hers? Perhaps their windows aren't as clean.

Sitting in the kitchen, Emily and Lavinia are shelling peas that roll like marbles between their fingers. On one side is a stoneware bowl filled with little round green peas: on the other are the plump pods. The empty hulls are piled on a clean cloth.

'If I could eat just one vegetable my entire life, it would be peas,' Lavinia says suddenly.

Emily agrees – not that she particularly likes peas, but the idea of eating just one thing *her entire life* seems restful.

Everyone agrees that Emily Dickinson had only one sister, Lavinia, known as Vinnie, born two years after her elder sister. But in reality, she has three other sisters, hidden in her bedroom: Anne, Charlotte, and Emily, like her. The Brontës live there in harmony with the rest of Emily's family: Browning, Emerson, and Thoreau.

Emily, who would rather not go to mass, gets down on her knees every morning before the flowers. She doesn't like weeding; unwanted plants are as good as any other, and she lets them grow in the midst of the ones she has planted. The garden is only half hers: the other half is the work of the bees.

Emily greets each plant by name, as if calling to young girls in hushed tones: Iris, Rose, Carolina, Lily, Daisy, Dahlia, Jasmine. The flowers answer her by giving her her own name: Emily, *aemula,* rival. She is the whitest of the lilies. Emily, absent from all earthly banquets.

In Scarborough, at the edge of the Atlantic Ocean, there is a road that is one of the most beautiful in all of New England. The large homes that face the ocean are pale, with cedar shingles and windows that reflect the sky or the sea. The ocean stretches before them, as far as the eye can see, beyond the tufted dunes and beach with sand so fine it is like golden sugar; behind them, beyond the road, there is only woods and swamps. These houses stand on the border between two types of wilderness, which, in a way, is the very definition of a home: a haven, *havene*, a port, and a refuge.

I could never live there. The name of the road is Massacre Lane. It's not that I'm afraid of the ghost of Richard 'Crazy Eye' Stonewall, who, it is said, has haunted the area since he was buried there in 1697, avenging his wife and infant, who were massacred by Native Americans a few years earlier. Nor do I fear the ghosts of dozens of colonists who tried and failed to defend the area of Prouts Neck against attacks by the same Native Americans, eighteen of whom died doing so in 1703. But I cannot read the word *massacre* ten times a day, on incoming or outgoing envelopes, forms, delivery slips, and road maps. I could not say it to friends and family who come to visit, spell it for vendors, repeat it ten times a week. It seems that what troubles me more than the massacre, or the massacres, is that their name has both replaced them (and, in a way, obliterated them) and proliferated them (which is to say, in a way, perpetuated them). To me, all streets are first paper streets.

The house we found, not far from there, also stands facing the ocean, in a village where the streets have the names Shell, Pearl, Shipwreck, Vesper, Morning.

I knew we were home when I walked through the door. As soon as you go in, you see the ocean and the sky through the large dining room windows. The view is the same from the bedroom on the second floor: the sand, the water, and the sky with, to the right, like a study in perspective, the crooked cedar-shingle homes of Bay Street shrinking in the distance. Barely visible on the horizon, beyond Prouts Neck, is the low profile of Biddeford. It is like looking down the coast from the top of a lighthouse.

We had the furniture, as well as the boxes with the things bought for the Boston apartment and left in storage for two years, delivered after we decided to make Outremont our home again, with a second home on the coast.

I unwrapped each object with some astonishment, as if they all belonged to strangers; for a few months, we had this other mysterious life. In one box was a diaper pail; in another were supplies for washing baby bottles: brushes, a drying rack, and soap. I looked at my daughter, who was playing among the boxes that filled the living room. She was three years old. The baby the objects were meant for was gone.

The cricket and the little print were in the last box. The title of the print wasn't *True North,* as I had thought, but *True Azimuth,* which is not the same thing, an azimuth being the measurement of the angle between the direction of a given object and a reference direction, most often magnetic north.

It is intrinsically a difference, an oblique line, that exists only in relation to another thing it is moving away from.

Tell all the truth but tell it slant, wrote Emily Dickinson, who also hated travel.

I put the cricket above the fireplace. It had finally found its home.

Mahogany furniture is good company: solid, faithful, silent.

On the walls climb roses, poor cousins of the garden roses – they lack the perfume, the velvety petals, the morning dew. Plus, the artist forgot to paint the thorns.

Emily goes around to all the windows to make sure they are open a crack – enough to fit two, not three, fingers, enough to let in the smell of lily of the valley, but not of a skunk. She draws the curtains just a little. The moon is almost full, a silver coin three quarters old.

She lets out one of Lavinia's cats who was lounging on a kitchen chair, right near the butter dish. She straightens the books with their gilded edges on the fireplace mantle, kneels to check that the embers are warm.

On her night table she places her oil lamp, a pitcher of water, and Emerson's poems. With her toe, she feels under the bed for the chamber pot. With the door shut, the universe is closed, sealed. She is ready to set sail.

When she gets up in the night to shut the window, the floorboards creak quietly under her feet.

She knows each one by name: *do, re, mi, fa, sol, la, ti, do* – C, D, E, F, G, A, B, C.

She often wakes up to write letters that she didn't get to during the day. She writes missives of ten, eight, seven lines, infinitely light, as if they were destined to travel in a sparrow's claws.

The goose feather scratching the paper brings to mind a mouse shelling a nut to get to the almond. The sound keeps the lamplight company, while the house sleeps, in the eclipse that separates night from morning. Emily never feels less alone than in the hours she spends bent over the paper, the goose's memory in hand, the imaginary mouse in a corner, her lamp oil taken from a gigantic whale, and the ink – the ink that comes from the fabulous belly of an underwater creature with eight arms. Before anything is written, the ink already evokes wonder.

In her lifetime, only a handful of her poems would be published, most often anonymously, after being heavily edited. She had long decided that *to write* is not only an intransitive verb, it is an end in itself. Why publish, if not for the base satisfaction of seeing one's name in print in a book or the newspaper, using the same lead characters that spelled those of Byron and Shakespeare. For the empty pleasure of knowing that hundreds of thousands of pairs of strange eyes will come to rest – with indifference or curiosity – on your words, which can only come through this ordeal sullied, or worn.

Do writers ever write for others, those real beings that Emily spies through her window, going about their business: driving their teams, concluding contracts, trading cattle, and selling off fabric? Or do they write for an idea of the Other, disembodied and sovereign, that the soul constructs, like a magnifying mirror, as it dreams of itself?

Emily has long been imagining this Reader, like most of the girls from Mount Holyoke imagined their Prince Charming or a rich fiancé. She sees this Master as superior to her in every way: more enlightened, nobler, greater. Only he knows how to truly appreciate her poetry. It turns out he is the editor-in-chief of a journal that publishes poetry? No matter.

In the meantime, her poems scratched out on packaging, cards, and envelopes continue to pile up in her drawers, forming fragile paper castles.

'Emily! There's a surprise for you!'

From Lavinia's tone, she assumes it must be a letter, perhaps accompanying a package – possibly a book?

She leaves her bedroom with her heart pounding, and in three steps she is at the top of the stairs, when she hears the guest's voice.

'Someone is here to see you!' Lavinia says.

Her heart clenches and races as if it has been betrayed. It is a surprise indeed, but a dreadful one. She wanted to delicately open the envelope alone in the silence of her bedroom, take out the paper, breathe it in before unfolding it, then bring her eyes to it, scanning the words once, twice, rereading them out of order, lying down while holding the letter to her chest as the words continue to flutter behind her closed eyes, and now she is required to face someone in the flesh, his boots no doubt still covered with mud from the road, and she will have to smile, ask questions, pretend to listen to the answers, all the while anticipating the happiness of finding herself alone to write him or reread one of his old missives. On tiptoe, she steps backward to her bedroom, making sure the floorboards don't creak. She closes the door behind her. Carlo looks up at his mistress. Dogs have a huge advantage over men that men cannot make up for: they don't talk.

'I very much enjoyed your ... short texts,' begins the man standing outside her door. She has made the mistake – she knows it as soon as he opens his mouth, which is large and filled with many teeth – of sending a few poems, in the hopes, not that he publish them, but that he see them in their true light.

She nods her head tentatively, a gesture as devoid of meaning as the polite words of the man speaking to her.

How could she have thought he would be able to read her work? And more importantly, how it is that men always fall short of their photos, their articles, and their letters? But Emily knows the answer to the question: she has grown fond of the paper beings, and they bear no relationship to the upright citizens she later discovers, men with their shoes, moustaches, asthma, stench of garlic, and suspenders. For years, she has tried to turn herself into a paper creature – to stop eating, sweating, and bleeding, to be someone who only reads and writes.

The man before her clears his throat. Is it too early to thank him for his visit and turn on her heel?

'There are, indeed, interesting images, although sometimes, how can I say ...'

She almost wants to rescue him, he seems so uncomfortable, but she is fuming, not so much at him as at herself, for letting herself once again, foolishly, hope.

'... a bit obscure, or complicated? Does a young woman like you really need to draw on a scientific vocabulary? And what exactly does it mean, *circumference*? Do you really need to use *axioms*, and *philology*? Wouldn't it be better to talk about feelings, rather than mathematics?'

Emily's silence seems to embolden him. He continues, in a tone he hopes is good-natured.

'And when it comes down to it, why call your writing poetry, if it is prose?'

This is too much. Emily starts in horror.

'What makes you say that?' Her voice is composed.

Embarrassed, he scratches his chin, where a few thick hairs grow. How is it that she keeps forgetting that men are hairy animals?

'Well, quite simply, it doesn't rhyme.'

So that's it. In a flash, Emily remembers a lesson from Mrs. Lyon about perfect and imperfect rhymes. *Cat, hat. Fish, dish. Love, dove.* Utter foolishness.

She who cares nothing about perfection or imperfection knows no other rhymes than those that are oblique or hanging – as they should be.

She rises calmly, nods to her visitor, and leaves. It doesn't rhyme. She can't help but smile.

The world. The world is as small as an orange. It is incredibly complicated and absolutely simple. The world can be replaced, recreated, annihilated by words. It exists on the other side of the window, which is another way of saying it doesn't exist at all. What does exist: the flame of the candle, the dog at her feet, the cotton sheets, the jasmine flowers pressed between the pages of dictionaries, sleeping between the words *daisy* and *day*, the embers in the hearth, the poems that throb in the drawer. The world is black and the bedroom is white. The poems are what bring it light.

The dressmaker rings the doorbell at the appointed time. She has been expecting her, and in just a few steps she reaches the door. The tea is already on the table. The two women exchange pleasantries, the living, the dead, the newly born; they haven't seen each other in months. Then they go upstairs.

'Perhaps you would like something different this year?' the dressmaker asks, laying out her measuring tape, fabric, chalk, a pencil, and some tissue paper.

'No, exactly the same thing.'

The dressmaker looks up. Her customer is undressing behind a Japanese screen on which peacocks fan their tails. She can see only the top of her head and her pale arms that lift to remove her shift.

'A bit of colour, perhaps?' she says.

The woman emerges from behind the screen in a corset and petticoat. The dressmaker hurries to take her measurements – shoulders, bust, waist, hips, arms, back, all the same as last year.

'Just white. Three of the same dress.'

'All three in white?' The dressmaker seems to resign herself with regret, as if she were being asked to do something contrary to her art.

'All three in white,' the woman confirms; she is already getting dressed again.

The dressmaker sighs, putting away her tools. She takes a sip of tea, which barely warms her. Lavinia sees her to the door, while, upstairs, Emily has not left her bedroom. The dresses will be a little large around the bust, the sleeves will be too short, because she and her sister aren't quite the same size.

If only she could also see to it that Lavinia were loved in her stead, she would be completely free.

The trees twist in the wind like flames. Emily would like to see the great hand of God, who is deigning for a moment to turn His attention to Earth. But when she looks up, she sees only that night is falling.

It takes her a little while to notice that things are starting to grow dim, and longer still to accept that it is because of her failing eyesight, not just the fruit of her imagination or the fact that the lamps aren't bright enough. But the pain, which is undeniable, keeps her up at night.

The Amherst doctor refers her to a specialist, an ophthalmologist in Boston, the capital, a six-hour journey, the end of the world.

❧

In the room next to the doctor's office, three women from polite Boston society are waiting, so alike that they could be cousins, even sisters, with their square jaws, their blue eyes, their polite smiles, and their flawless bodices. Emily, who feels like a stranger everywhere in this city, feels more than ever like a dog among cats.

The door opens; it's her turn. The doctor is short; he has round glasses, a bald head, and a small paunch. He is properly terrifying.

He examines Emily, asks her questions, listens to her chest. She tries her best to describe the pain. Words fail her. He shines a light in her eyes, asks her to read rows of meaningless letters, increasingly small, then he examines her again, this time without speaking. She awaits his verdict like a guillotine blade.

'I don't think ...' he begins, then he coughs quietly. 'I don't think you are going to lose your sight.'

Emily exhales.

'But the problem is quite advanced,' he says, 'and your eyes are in great need of rest. If you want to have any hope of healing, you have to give up reading and writing for two, perhaps three, months.'

Emily stops breathing. Her sight has been restored only to have her wind taken away.

But he isn't done.

'I recommend you not travel during that time. It would be better for you to stay in Boston.'

She returns to her cousins' home with a heavy heart, forcing herself not to read what is written on signs or in store windows, to practise living without words.

Far from home, with no books, Emily spends two months in the dark – an exile twice over.

When she returns to Amherst at last, she takes the stairs four at a time, shuts her bedroom door behind her, and opens Shakespeare's *Sonnets*. Finally, she is home.

As a child, she was happy to put flowers in books written by others. As an adult, she takes on bigger challenges: birds and clouds that, traced on a white page, keep threatening to fly away, leaving you alone with your desire.

One day, she decides to slip some of her poems into an envelope addressed to Thomas Wentworth Higginson, accompanied by this plea: *Are you too deeply occupied to say if my verse is alive?*

One could imagine the man deciphering them, astonished, then carefully weighing his response. When he asks her in a letter who are her companions, Emily replies: *Hills, sir, and the sundown, and a dog large as myself, that my father bought me.* And, of course, *The Apocalypse.*

Do not publish, Higginson told her, after reading her poetry, and this advice, which would dismay many, delights her. Publish, for what? She does not want to – and has never wanted to – make books, which are heavy, eternal, smelling of cigars and stuffiness. The few poems she has dispatched into the world have appeared on the flimsy sheets of newspapers, which live only one day, ephemeral.

She writes on paper, but that is because she was never able to put together an album big enough to contain the spring showers and the autumn wind – there is no herbarium for snow. She dreams of poems written with insects, which would start walking around on their long legs, their carapaces shining like armour against the self-righteous and extraordinarily proper ladies who shriek when they see a ladybug. No doubt the ladybugs are also shrieking at these petticoat towers topped by parasols, but they cannot be heard: they are the true ladies.

She dreams of poems that could be read in the stars, if only we could finally learn the language of their faint constellations. She dreams of complicated odes to circuits and mathematical circumferences. Of the golden sonnets bees trace in honey. Of those that Our Lord God would have written to pass the time, on the seventh day of Creation, if only He existed.

Do not publish. Your writing is much too precious for that. Keep it for you, and you alone. And for me, perhaps.

A tiny creature appears. She seems to hover a few inches above the ground. The man wonders for a moment whether she is on casters, given how quickly and smoothly she is advancing. Dressed in white, she has a thin face, shining eyes, and slightly stilted movements. In each hand she holds a white lily, which she offers him, and whispers, 'By way of introduction.'

He doesn't know how to respond and stands there, the large flowers in his hands, while she looks at him, her face slightly tilted, like a bird ready to take flight. He bows. When he straightens up, she is gone.

That evening, he will detail the encounter in a letter to his wife. She will admonish him for not having kept the flowers.

Higginson is a wise man. Too often, she loathes wise people. Emily far prefers the company of butterflies, grasshoppers, and books – which are also wise, but quiet. They do not overwhelm you with their wisdom. They wait for you to pluck them when you are ready.

He pictures these poems that she calls *snow* as delicate, airborne snowflakes, almost supernaturally fragile – the finest lace made of words. But in writing *snow*, what Emily sees in her mind's eye is the most powerful avalanche.

She steps out in silence when the house is asleep. The street is calm under the tall trees. She walks for a few minutes, arrives in front of his house. A lamp is shining in his bedroom window. She enters without knocking.

He undresses her slowly, removing layer after layer, like peeling an onion, the armour of fabric that women are burdened with: skirt, petticoat, corset, chemise. He slowly kisses her shoulders, her breasts, her stomach. She undresses him in turn; they wrap themselves around each other under the sheets without blowing out the candle. Their familiar scents blend into a single musky aroma, sweet and pungent, the smell of damp fur. They know each other as water knows the ground.

When they are done, she wipes her thigh.

He asks, for the hundredth time, 'Will you marry me?'

For the hundredth time, Lavinia answers, 'No.'

She already has enough to do.

Emily sits in her chair in front of the window. There is almost nothing going on. The sky, the trees, the Evergreens not far off, the chirp of the crickets. Night falls. Everything is plunged in ink. The moon appears, hunched in the middle of the sky. Her heart slowly tears in her chest. There is almost nothing going on.

I still don't know if I will go visit Homestead, as I try to picture the walls hung with floral wallpaper, the creaking floors, the windows on the second floor overlooking Main Street, and the November garden.

If, at the end of the tour, rather than sensibly following the guide, I hid under a bed or slipped behind a door – and if I stayed there until evening, waiting for everyone to go home, to come out of my hiding spot, go to the window in the dark, and observe the remains of the garden rigid in the first fall frost – then I would have the night all to myself.

What is Emily waiting for, at age thirty, forty, fifty? Love? God? A blue jay? Someone who will finally read her poems the way she dreamed they would be read? Or simply death, which she wards off every day by writing a few more words, fragile incantations that create tiny flickers – fireflies – in the dark.

My business is circumference, Emily wrote. And she does indeed seem to be constantly teetering on the verge of things, a well or the abyss, between one world and another, on the threshold between the poem and the indescribable, an apple in hand, a foot in the grave.

Emily Dickinson's manuscripts are conserved at Harvard University's Houghton Library, where you can't actually see them, but you can handle facsimiles, along with copies of letters addressed to her correspondents. There is also a room called simply the Dickinson Room, which contains a range of objects (furniture, books, and carpets) that belonged to the family. You can visit the room, which is not a real bedroom, every Friday at two p.m.

Seeing the herbarium is out of the question – it is too fragile. The leaves of the trees, like the leaves of the book, could turn to dust. The library provides replicas, copies.

While we lived in Boston, twice we went to visit the tract of land that is Harvard. Shaded by mature trees, its red-brick buildings are so familiar from films that you feel like you are walking through a movie set populated by extras hired to look like students. Even the ivy clinging to the buildings, which has lent its name to the prestigious Ivy League schools – among them, Harvard, Yale, Princeton, and Dartmouth – seems to have been placed there to add colour.

The first time I visited, I ended up taking refuge in the huge campus library, with floor-to-ceiling shelves. Only the books were real.

❧

I was twenty-five when I was sent to spend a few days in Ottawa to consult Gabrielle Roy's manuscripts, conserved in the National Library archives. I had been hired, along with a small team of master's and doctoral students, to prepare the publication of the next installment of *Enchantment and Sorrow,* Roy's unfinished autobiography, no doubt her most famous work – my favourite, at any rate.

Twenty years later, I can still clearly remember the day when I first held in my white-gloved hands the notebooks in which she handwrote the dozens of pages that would become *Le temps qui m'a manqué.* I never went to visit her home in Petite-Rivière-Saint-François and felt no particular emotion when passing the Château Saint-Louis on Grande Allée in Quebec City, where for years she lived in an apartment with her husband. I have never collected author memorabilia – whether first editions, signed copies, or other rarities. Yet I remember, that morning, being swept over by an emotion that caught me off guard. I was holding in my hands something as fragile as a butterfly wing, yet that had travelled through time. These few sheets were Gabrielle Roy's true home, the building she had worked to build until her last breath, and that she left unfinished, but standing.

If I don't go to Amherst, the only place where I can encounter or visit Emily is in her house of poems. But she and I do not speak the same language: hers is poetry, mine is prose.

Poetry is always a foreign language. For those who speak and read French, English poetry is doubly foreign, a strange country twice over.

First, you know nothing. Then you know what you don't know – half the journey travelled.

Then the words and images come back in a loop. You encounter them again as if in half-forgotten dreams, the meaning of them still escaping you. They teach you what they mean. They draw closer to their readers, cautiously, to tame them. Soon, you are wandering through poems like a forest, still just as mysterious, but the shadowy light is broken by trails and rays of sun. Soon, you start to inhabit the forest, recognizing birds and creatures, black ponds, and towering oaks. Soon, the forest starts to grow inside you.

After fifty, Austin does the unthinkable for a Dickinson: he takes a mistress. Twenty-five years his junior. Mabel is lively, pretty, brilliant, and married. Her husband is an astronomer who barely raises an eyebrow at the liaison, but Susan is devastated upon reading, in Austin's journal, the day after he spends the evening alone with the young woman, the word *Rubicon*.

There are fewer lamps shining in the windows at Evergreens. After sunset, the house is plunged in darkness. Love has taken its light somewhere else.

It has been over two years that Emily has been dressing only in white, the colour of the curious snowflake-poems she has been collecting in her drawers without really sharing them, as if she feared they would melt in any hands other than her own. Meanwhile, Lavinia has grown darker. From lilac, her dresses have turned to plum, then brown, and soon she will dress only in black, wearing yesterday's mourning and tomorrow's death at once.

She jealously guards the solitude of her older sister, who, in town, people have started to call, with an admiration tinged with mockery, Queen Recluse. Or the Myth.

She announces to an unexpected visitor who shows up one morning freshly shaven, a bouquet of violets in hand, that Emily will not be coming down.

'No matter,' the visitor says. 'I will go up.'

Lavinia jumps. Perched at the top of the steps, Emily jumps too.

'Go up, the very thought!' Lavinia says. 'But if you would like to take tea in the parlour, you are most welcome.'

And she goes into the kitchen with the violets, to put the kettle on. Emily hears hesitant steps heading toward the parlour before doubling back and starting up the stairs.

She dashes to her bedroom and closes the door behind her. The visitor stops on the other side of the door and announces, 'I have come to talk about your poetry.'

If he thought he had found a key that would magically open the door, he could have spared himself the trouble. Emily answers from behind the closed door.

'Well then, talk.'

Suddenly he is at a loss for words, which rarely happens. In truth, he would have liked to have asked her about her strange poems, which contain equal parts silence and words and which bring to mind – he doesn't really know why – coded messages slipped into bottles tossed to the whims of the seas. He sits on the floor. A ray of light filters under the door. Downstairs, Lavinia calls him, but he doesn't answer.

He asks the ray of golden light, 'Why do you not want to publish them?'

But that is not quite what he wanted to ask. What he doesn't understand is why this curious woman agreed to show him poems and then vehemently refuses to make them public. Why him? It's actually not so much Emily's poetry he wants to discuss, but Emily.

On the other side of the door, Emily has withdrawn. She has taken her place near the window. Her heart has stopped racing. When it races again, it is because she sees the red flash of a cardinal in the leaves of a maple.

At her window, Emily hangs a hemp rope that sways gently in the wind.

It is not to serve as a ladder for squirrels, even though a number of them have tried to climb it, nor is it to let her slip unnoticed to the ground by the light of the moon – although she has often dreamed of it. It is to lower, in a wicker basket lined with a pristine white handkerchief, an army of little gingerbread men to her nieces and nephew, who are waiting down below. We aren't surprised that Emily Dickinson is a baker, so why be surprised to learn she is an aunt?

Because people think poets don't have families, but that is just not true, of course. Poets are daughters, sisters, cousins. It is the poem that is the orphan.

Of Austin and Susan's three children, Gilbert, the youngest and the only boy, is Emily's favourite. Blond locks, eyes as round as saucers, he walks at gladiola height and is filled with wonder at everything he discovers: a nest that has fallen from a tree, a caterpillar with long blue bristles, a dog's paw print in the dirt. With their thousand green eyes, the trees listen to them talking, the tall spinster dressed in white leaning out her window and the child on his tricycle looking up toward the sky.

With her nephew, Emily is seeing the world through fresh eyes. With his aunt, Gilbert is seeing it for one of the last times. They don't know it yet – but the trees, well, they have their suspicions.

There is no sense looking for a turning point or crossroads in Emily Dickinson's life. For decades, people have been trying to unearth – or even manufacture – a significant event, a trauma, a love story gone wrong – with a man or a woman, either way – a betrayal, or some madness that would explain the strange isolation in which she chose to spend the second half of her life. Minds that crave symmetry want to understand a before and an after, separated by misfortune, tragedy, or revelation. We want to read the landscape of her life like a mountain, the summit of which is the culmination, the centre, and the fulcrum. But as deep as one might dig, writing biographies, poring over letters and eyewitness accounts, no such event can be found. There is no catastrophe, no tipping point, no rupture. Emily's withdrawal is gradual. Maybe quite simply, like most people who, as they age, grow more set in their ways and become more profoundly themselves, she gave into her natural penchant: solitude, and its corollary, silence. It isn't really that hard to imagine. When you think about it, it is hard to understand why more writers don't make the same choice.

She is not hiding; she is not a recluse. She is at the essence of things, deep inside herself, contemplative, perched in equilibrium between the bees in the garden and the two Dippers, big and little, that light up in the sky when the sun goes down, outstretched like the stylus on a sundial.

It is an ideal life, ideally hermetic, enclosed. Round and full like an egg. Every day comes full circle, one that begins with the sun appearing above the treetops, golden in summer, copper in autumn, mercury in winter, pink in spring, and ends with its disappearance at the other end of the sky. The dark night: a blank. The next morning, the same, but never really.

It is in this exquisite repetition of things, in this time suspended, that she manages, in flashes, to understand what the grass is murmuring and the wind is whispering. There is no way to stop, other than to turn at exactly the same speed as the Earth circling the Sun, and to give in to the vertigo.

The autumn doesn't need us. It is self-sufficient, with its lavish golds and bronzes. It has so much that it tosses its riches on the ground in a fit of laughter. It knows that summer is short and death is long.

Emily cracks the window, and her breath is almost taken away. The perfumes go to her head. The world has grown more intense since she started contemplating it from her bedroom above. As if the window concentrated the colours, like the first camera, the camera obscura. To see it even better, to soak it all in, you would have to look at it through the keyhole.

It is untrue that she has only her bedroom. She has the song of the starlings, the inky black of November nights, spring showers, familiar voices that rise up from below with the smell of bread baking, the scent of the apple blossoms, the heat of stones warmed by the sun at the end of the day, all things we miss after death.

Year in and year out, the radius of her revolutions grows shorter, like a rope that, as it turns, imperceptibly coils around its axis. Year in and year out, she draws closer to the heart: the bedroom, the desk, the inkwell. The world will end up perched on the tip of the pen she holds in her hand.

In Emily's hand, the pen writes on its own. It tells the story of the bird, from an egg in the hollow of the nest to its first tentative flight, the green light of summer level with a blade of grass, the crispness of autumn, the long migration south, the return to the spring. The pen tells of all this to whomever knows how to bring the paper to her ear like a shell. Emily, who despite herself can glimpse the beginning and the end of all things, cannot see an infant without imagining the old man he will become, and likewise, when seeing an old man, can clearly make out the baby he doesn't remember having been.

For a moment, she lifts the pen from the paper because it has run out of ink. Rather than dipping it in the inkwell, she gently places the silver tip in the centre of her palm. The pen traces the lines of her hand: heart, life, money, snail.

Mother has an attack that leaves her diminished, weakened, as if subdued. She can still get around and speak, but she does so with hesitation, as if she has a hard time remembering how. She spends most of her days in bed. Sometimes she confuses her two daughters or doesn't recognize them at all. Lavinia and Emily take care of the invalid day and night, feed her, groom her, read to her.

Every morning, Emily enters Mother's bedroom with a breakfast tray: eggs, porridge, fresh bread, tea with milk. She opens the curtains, tells her what the weather is like, props her up on pillows, and patiently feeds her with a small silver spoon.

Emily, who said she never had a mother – *I always ran Home to Awe when a child, if anything befell me. He was an awful Mother, but I liked him better than none* – suddenly finds herself with a daughter.

At the break of dawn, Emily is awoken by pealing bells. A clamour rises from the street, agitation combined with the stamping of horses' hooves, the cries of men, and what sound like distant explosions.

Lavinia comes into her bedroom almost immediately, in a nightdress, her hair down.

'Don't worry. It's the Fourth of July, remember?'

Emily agrees solemnly. Since the situation is so dire that it requires she be lied to, she will go along with it.

'Of course,' she says. 'I had forgotten.' Then, 'Maybe we should go to Mother's bedroom, so she doesn't worry.'

The sisters go sit at the end of the invalid's bed, and she doesn't awaken all morning, while outside the bells keep ringing, and the cavalcade of horses and the screams continue. A strong smell of smoke filters through the closed windows as they play cards. Lavinia braids Emily's hair into a crown. They take turns reading Bible verse, challenging each other to name the passage. At the beginning of the afternoon, when the unrest has died down, they go down to the kitchen to make eggs for lunch.

'You see, it was just the Fourth of July,' Lavinia says, while at the other end of town the embers of the general store and seven houses are still smoking.

If the wind had been blowing in the other direction, Emily thought, as she heated the water for tea, there would be nothing left of us. Paper burns so quickly.

While doing renovations in Outremont last year, we discovered, when tearing out a riser between the dinette and the dining room that was added to the house some forty years after it was built, a dozen little cards starting to yellow, each one depicting a saint. A little larger than playing cards, and pastel-coloured, they made up a curious family, reminiscent of the circus, the Church, and caravans of wanderers.

They featured Our Lady of Fátima; Our Lady of the Cape, palms upturned, feet bare, wreathed in stars, wearing a robe with gilded motifs and a domed crown; St. Anthony of Padua, the patron saint of lost things; Andrew the Apostle; Our Lady of Mount Carmel; the Supreme Pontiff at prayer (it was Pope Pius XII, reciting the prayer of the Jubilee year 1950 for the first time); a card with the Mother Most Admirable on the back, a host of cherubs watching over her, and Our Lady of Perpetual Help on the front. The other cards depict Christ on the cross, the holy child in the manger, the Resurrection, Jesus preaching to children and, on a card long and thin like a finger, a little blond child with his arms full of flowers.

I can't say I was surprised to see this little clan emerge from the plaster. I always knew we weren't alone here.

When people ask me where I live, I specify Outremont rather than Montreal (Montreal being more accurate after the municipal mergers a few years ago, and better known, at least among foreigners) because it feels to me that Outremont is still too big. I live on a street, in two parks, and on the neighbouring mountain. Once I am on Van Horne, I'm no longer at home, no more than on Hutchison or Laurier. My Outremont is tiny, its streets uniformly lined with red-brick houses from the turn of the last century. I long had the impression, when walking Victor the Great Dane, and later Zoé in her stroller, that the original residents who watched us go by looked slightly perplexed. My Outremont is right at the junction of 1917 (the year my house was built) and 2017 (the year I write these lines), a bit like one of those mirrors that swing open when light pressure is applied, to reveal a secret passage in a wall, a hidden cabinet, or another mirror.

What I left in going to Boston was a past I hadn't experienced but that I lived in nonetheless: the eighty summers and winters of our maple tree, and the little paper people living undetected within our walls.

The maple was cut down two years ago almost to the day, after coming close to taking off the roof of the house one evening of freezing rain and high winds. Small white mushrooms gradually colonized the stump. We will probably have it removed and plant a new tree. But I still write to the shadow of the ghost of the maple.

I remember being acutely aware as a child of living in a child town.

We moved to Rue de la Rivière, in Cap-Rouge, shortly after I was born; the street hadn't existed a few years earlier. We lived in a little prefab house where no one had lived before us, which alone astonished me: the house had been assembled indoors (inside a larger house?), like a toy building made of wooden blocks. Nothing existed before, and that was disorienting.

Nothing tied us to the place; at any moment we could have blown away forever. And yet, at the time, I must have known that under the ground, my sister was sleeping in her coffin.

Her bedroom had been transformed into a room we called the den, where we watched TV, generally in silence. From time to time, an electric shock ran through me. She had lived here, dreamed here, and no trace of that remained. Vanished. Silence.

As a child, I tried, with books, homes, paintings, and shells, to scratch the surface and find out what lay dormant below. Because below this world there must be something else, which evaded the eye and had to be gently excavated, like unearthing the fragile ruins of buried cities with a very fine brush.

Emily has long stopped leaving the garden, then the house, eventually remaining shut away in her bedroom almost the entire day. When visitors call, she sometimes receives them, but from behind a screen. They sit on a chair in a deserted room, she takes her place on the other side of the partition, and each person speaks to the wall.

Visitors are few and far between, even more so return visitors. No one likes going to confession. And yet, this curious intimacy with one who is absent prompts more than one person to express thoughts they didn't even know they had, and they leave a little ashamed, with the vague sense of having been fooled, but not knowing by whom.

To ask forgiveness, Emily gives visitors tiny gifts as a child would have imagined them: a sprig of lily of the valley, a rosebud, pristine white clover, sometimes a few verses, or a glass of golden sherry.

She stops going out, but she does not abandon her garden. The garden joins her in the bedroom: that's where it blooms now. People are presumptuous in their astonishment that Emily has chosen to live among the flowers.

People are amazed at her later years spent in solitude, as if it were a superhuman feat, but, I repeat, what is astonishing is that more don't do it, writers shutting themselves quietly away at home to write. Isn't it rather the circus of ordinary life, with its endless trivialities and obligations, that is superhuman? Why be amazed that someone who lives primarily through books should choose to sacrifice contact with her fellow creatures? You would have to have a high opinion of yourself indeed to want to be constantly surrounded by those who resemble you.

She would have liked to make a book with only flowers, like she did at age fourteen. But now she lives in a white garden. She pins words on paper like butterflies. Her pen scratches like a bird. Her poems are at least one-half chickadee. The other half contains asters, the fiery breast of sunsets, eternity's vast pocket, the countless hordes from the bible that dreams near her bed.

I dwell in Possibility —
A fairer House than Prose —
More numerous of Windows —
Superior — for Doors —

Three long letters to an unnamed Master survived the passage of time and the relatives and publishers who went through Emily's affairs. Were these drafts of three frenzied, breathless missives that were sent to their intended recipient, or did Emily write them and decide to keep them for herself? Or did she write them knowing they were not meant to be sent, that she was not writing to a real recipient? As with everything else, the clues are so flimsy and sparse that people can choose the explanation that suits them. My take: the Master didn't exist.

She wanted to invent him, couldn't quite, and never forgave him.

When her drawers start to overflow with loose poems – cinnamon, chocolate, seeds, flour, and sugar – Emily sets out to assemble them into little books. She starts by spreading them on her desk to see them all before her. The wooden surface is soon covered. She stands, places a few poems on her chair, then on the mantle, then decides to put them on the floor, side by side, not touching, like pieces of a gigantic puzzle.

The poems fill the bedroom. She has to clear narrow channels between the pieces of paper and tiptoe around so as not to crumple them, advancing gingerly, as if she were walking on a frozen pond threatening to give way under her weight.

When she spreads all the poems out, she stands there, observing them. And if there's a gust of wind, or a spark?

She bends over, picks one at random, looks for its sibling or cousin. This is found on the other side of the room. Excellent. Now she has two in her hands. It is harder to find a third one that will not only tether itself to the second but also converse with the first in a sort of private conversation. The difficulty, obviously, increases with the number, and when, after two hours, Emily has gathered a bundle of some fifteen poems, she has grown dizzy as if after too much port. She carefully piles the remaining poems, putting them off until tomorrow.

But the task has grown even more complicated during the night, because now she no longer has the most eloquent and engaging poems, which gladly agree to strike up a friendship with the others, like jovial guests who put everyone at ease at a soirée. The more she advances, the more the remaining poems are daunting, prickly like chestnuts, resisting contact with their peers. Soon she is surrounded only by poems that are like her – a small assembly of loners.

A week passes before she has to face facts: she has to undo all the collections she has painfully created and start from scratch, which she does. And again in a few weeks, and then a few months later. It takes almost a year before she manages to find each one a family and a home.

She gathers the poems into fascicles a few dozen pages long. Then she borrows a sewing basket from Lavinia, threads a needle, puts a silver thimble on the end of her finger, and, with painstaking care, sews the little single-copy books one stitch at a time.

But the word *fascicle,* still used to describe the slim handwritten collections assembled in the privacy of her bedroom, means, first, in pharmacy, the quantity of plants one can hold in the crook of an arm with a hand resting on the hip, an estimated twelve handfuls.

Before becoming a book, a fascicle is an armful of healing plants.

To a correspondent who one day asks her how she knows when she is in the presence of poetry, she answers, *If I read a book and it makes my whole body so cold no fire can ever warm me I know that is poetry.* Then, *If I feel physically as if the top of my head were taken off, I know* that *is poetry. These are the only ways I know it. Is there any other way?*

One hundred and fifty years later, where Leonard Cohen would speak of ashes, Emily speaks of cold. Either way, a poem is the flip side of fire.

Death inhabits all poems, and not only death but Dying, the Supreme Moment, suspended, too, like the rhymes in her poems – like snowflakes in a storm that seem to rise back up to the sky once they are halfway down, already missing the clouds; like time stopping with June sunsets; like a hanged man swinging, livid, at the end of his rope.

In quick succession, barely one year apart, Father goes to sleep in the cemetery, and Mother joins him. Lavinia and Emily are alone in the big house now, Lavinia with her cats and Emily with her dog. They have a servant, Margaret, who has no pets.

Her father is dead, but Emily never goes to sit by his grave. You can weep for the dead anywhere, but Emily doesn't cry. One day, a friend goes to the cemetery and in the grass near the gravestone picks a four-leaf clover, which she gives to Emily. Emily solemnly accepts the gift and spends a long time after the visitor has left contemplating the little green cross. Then she places the clover to dry between the pages of the complete works of Shakespeare, which already has a dozen of them – her own little cemetery.

People say that during this time in her life she had a great love, maybe the only one of her existence. Judge Otis Phillips Lord, an old friend of her father's and some fifteen years her senior, assiduously courted her, and she responded with letters filled with emotion. Was marriage truly a possibility between them? Did Emily really think about leaving Amherst to go live in Salem, the land of her cousins, the witches? Or was she trying to invent a life on paper one last time? Almost nothing remains of their romance – their letters were destroyed, leaving only the odd draft, stories passed down through the generations of the two families. The fiancé died before the marriage could be celebrated, consummated, or even announced. Emily would never be a widow.

She has reached an age where there are more dead than living in one's circle of acquaintance. Sophia, Father, Mother, and Gilbert with the blond curls are resting under the green grass. The earth may be depopulating, but the heavens seem no less empty.

And yet, you can be sure, seated at the long, heavenly table, Father and Mother, looking as stern as ever, await their children – who are late once again.

For the past few days, as soon as she puts her head on the pillow, she hears bells. After having spent her life doubting the existence of God, she now has a cathedral in her head.

She has always had the sense of being followed. As a little girl, she would sit on the piano bench, her legs dangling, play a few notes to attract her pursuer, then turn around quickly. The Person wouldn't show herself. When she would stroll around the garden, she would stop for a moment near a tree, pressing herself against the trunk, staring at the path she had walked down. The Person still wouldn't show herself.

She walks behind Emily in the street, in the shadow of the houses; she follows her to the cellar when she goes to get potatoes. She sits at her side in the warm bathwater, she lies down with her between the cotton sheets, they both read from the same page, the same book. In one sense, it's good: Emily is never alone.

They are standing together facing the window. There is no moon, but the stars are so bright that she feels like she is looking at them through a magnifying glass. The stars form familiar drawings in the sky – it's a map with rivers, towns, and deserts. Somewhere up there, at the end of a road scattered with white pebbles, Linden shines.

Emily and her death take flight together. It is in the month of May.

On Emily Dickinson's death certificate, next to the word *occupation*, a perfectly precise hand has written: *At home.*

Linden

Linden is a city in green and blond – honey and clover.

In a small house with curtains drawn live Sophia and Gilbert, forever age fifteen and eight. They eat gingerbread cookies and drink warm milk for breakfast.

Dogs roam the streets, all the dogs who are loved and have died. The sea is always close by; you can hear it but never see it.

In Linden, Emily comes out of her bedroom, goes down the stairs, crosses the threshold of her paper house, and goes out into the street and the noonday sun, wearing a scarlet dress.

Author's Note

I borrowed the idea of comparing (albeit at different times) the populations of Amherst and Chicago from Roger Lundin, whose *Emily Dickinson and the Art of Belief* also provided me the substance of some of the episodes in the poet's life. Other moments are drawn from *The Life of Emily Dickinson,* by Richard B. Sewall, or episodes narrated by Emily Dickinson herself in her correspondence; others still are the fruit of my imagination. If readers cannot tell one from the other, so much the better.

Thank you to Nadine Bismuth, my first reader, and to François Ricard for his wisdom and his invaluable comments on the manuscript. Thank you to Antoine Tanguay for his trust and friendship for the past ten years. Thank you to Rafaële Germain for putting me on the track for parliaments of owls and kaleidoscopes of butterflies. Thank you to Alana Wilcox and Rhonda Mullins for giving my Emily a new life.

Dominique Fortier is a writer and translator living in Outremont, Quebec. Her first novel, *On the Proper Use of Stars,* was nominated for a Governor General's Award, and *Au péril de la mer* won the GG for French fiction. She is the author of six books, including most recently *The Island of Books.*

Rhonda Mullins has translated many books into English, including *The Island of Books* and Anaïs Barbeau-Lavalette's *Suzanne,* a Canada Reads finalist for 2019. She won the Governor General's Award for Translation for Jocelyne Saucier's *Twenty-One Cardinals.*

Typeset in Jenson

Printed at the Coach House on bpNichol Lane in Toronto, Ontario, on Zephyr Antique Laid paper, which was manufactured, acid-free, in Saint-Jérôme, Quebec, from second-growth forests. This book was printed with vegetable-based ink on a 1973 Heidelberg KORD offset litho press. Its pages were folded on a Baumfolder, gathered by hand, bound on a Sulby Auto-Minabinda, and trimmed on a Polar single-knife cutter.

Translated by Rhonda Mullins
Edited by Alana Wilcox
Cover design by Ingrid Paulson
Cover image from Emily Dickinson's Herbarium, courtesy of the Houghton Library, Harvard University (MS Am 1118.11)
Design by Crystal Sikma
Author photo by Frederick Duchesne
Translator photo by Owen Egan

Coach House Books
80 bpNichol Lane
Toronto ON M5S 3J4
Canada

416 979 2217
800 367 6360

mail@chbooks.com
www.chbooks.com